DEADEYE DICK

BY KURT VONNEGUT

A Man Without a Country
Armageddon in Retrospect
Bagombo Snuff Box
Between Time and Timbuktu
Bluebeard
Breakfast of Champions
Canary in a Cat House
Cat's Cradle
Deadeye Dick
Fates Worse Than Death
Galápagos
God Bless You, Dr. Kevorkian
God Bless You, Mr. Rosewater
Happy Birthday, Wanda June
Hocus Pocus
Jailbird
Like Shaking Hands with God (*with* Lee Stringer)
Look at the Birdie: Unpublished Short Fiction
Mother Night
Palm Sunday
Player Piano
The Sirens of Titan
Slapstick
Slaughterhouse-Five
Timequake
Wampeters, Foma & Granfalloons
Welcome to the Monkey House

DEADEYE DICK

KURT VONNEGUT

DIAL PRESS TRADE PAPERBACKS

2010 Dial Press Trade Paperback Edition

Published in the United States by Dial Press Trade Paperbacks, an imprint of The Random House Publishing Group, a division of Random House, Inc., New York.

DIAL PRESS and DIAL PRESS TRADE PAPERBACKS are registered trademarks of Random House, Inc., and the colophon is a trademark of Random House, Inc.

Originally published in hardcover in the United States by Delacorte Press/Seymour Lawrence, an imprint of The Random House Publishing Group, a division of Random House, Inc., in 1982.

ISBN 978-0-385-33417-4

Printed in the United States of America
Published simultaneously in Canada

www.dialpress.com

27

Cover illustration by Kurt Vonnegut. Copyright © 2005 Kurt Vonnegut/Origami Express, LLC. www.vonnegut.com

Book design by Nancy Field

The Kurt Vonnegut, Jr. Trust came into existence after the death of Kurt Vonnegut, Jr., and is committed to the continued protection of his works.

For Jill

PREFACE

"DEADEYE DICK," like "Barnacle Bill," is a nickname for a sailor. A deadeye is a rounded wooden block, usually bound with rope or iron, and pierced with holes. The holes receive a multiplicity of lines, usually shrouds or stays, on an old-fashioned sailing ship. But in the American Middle West of my youth, "Deadeye Dick" was an honorific often accorded to a person who was a virtuoso with firearms.

So it is a sort of lungfish of a nickname. It was born in the ocean, but it adapted to life ashore.

. . .

There are several recipes in this book, which are intended as musical interludes for the salivary glands. They have been inspired by *James Beard's American Cookery,* Marcella Hazan's *The Classic Italian Cook Book,* and Bea Sandler's *The African Cookbook.* I have tinkered with the originals, however—so no one should use this novel for a cookbook.

Any serious cook should have the reliable originals in his or her library anyway.

• • •

There is a real hotel in this book, the Grand Hotel Oloffson in Port au Prince, Haiti. I love it, and so would almost anybody else. My dear wife Jill Krementz and I have stayed there in the so-called "James Jones Cottage," which was built as an operating room when the hotel was headquarters for a brigade of United States Marines, who occupied Haiti, in order to protect American financial interests there, from 1915 until 1934.

The exterior of that austere wooden box has subsequently been decorated with fanciful, jigsaw gingerbread, like the rest of the hotel.

The currency of Haiti, by the way, is based on the American dollar. Whatever an American dollar is worth, that is what a Haitian dollar is worth, and actual American dollars are in general circulation. There seems to be no scheme in Haiti, however, for retiring worn-out dollar bills, and replacing them with new ones. So it is ordinary there to treat with utmost seriousness a dollar which is as insubstantial as a cigarette paper, and which has shrunk to the size of an airmail stamp.

I found one such bill in my wallet when I got home from Haiti a couple of years ago, and I mailed it back to Al and Sue Seitz, the owners and host and hostess of the Oloff-son, asking them to release it into its natural environment. It could never have survived a day in New York City.

. . .

James Jones (1921-1977), the American novelist, was actually married to his wife Gloria in the James Jones Cottage, before it was called that. So it is a literary honor to stay there.

There is supposedly a ghost—not of James Jones, but of somebody else. We never saw it. Those who have seen it describe a young white man in a white jacket, possibly a medical orderly of some kind. There are only two doors, a back door opening into the main hotel, and the front door opening onto a porch. This ghost is said to follow the same route every time it appears. It comes in through the back door, searches for something in a piece of furniture which isn't there anymore, and then goes out the front door. It vanishes when it passes through the front door. It has never been seen in the main hotel or on the porch.

It may have an uneasy conscience about something it did or saw done when the cottage was an operating room.

. . .

There are four real painters in this book, one living and three dead. The living one is my friend in Athens, Ohio, Cliff McCarthy. The dead ones are John Rettig, Frank Duveneck, and Adolf Hitler.

Cliff McCarthy is about my age and from my part of America, more or less. When he went to art school, it was drummed into him that the worst sort of painter was eclectic, borrowing from here and there. But now he has had a show of thirty years of his work, at Ohio University, and he says, "I notice that I have been eclectic." It's strong and lovely stuff he does. My own favorite is "The Artist's Mother as a Bride in 1917." His mother is all dressed up, and it's a warm time of year, and somebody has persuaded her to pose in the bow of a rowboat. The rowboat is in a perfectly still, narrow patch of water, a little river, probably, with the opposite bank, all leafy, only fifty yards away. She is laughing.

There really was a John Rettig, and his painting in the Cincinnati Art Museum, "Crucifixion in Rome," is as I have described it.

There really was a Frank Duveneck, and I in fact own a painting by him, "Head of a Young Boy." It is a treasure left to me by my father. I used to think it was a portrait of my brother Bernard, it looks so much like him.

And there really was an Adolf Hitler, who studied art in Vienna before the First World War, and whose finest picture may in fact have been "The Minorite Church of Vienna."

• • •

I will explain the main symbols in this book.

There is an unappreciated, empty arts center in the

shape of a sphere. This is my head as my sixtieth birthday beckons to me.

There is a neutron bomb explosion in a populated area. This is the disappearance of so many people I cared about in Indianapolis when I was starting out to be a writer. Indianapolis is there, but the people are gone.

Haiti is New York City, where I live now.

The neutered pharmacist who tells the tale is my declining sexuality. The crime he committed in childhood is all the bad things I have done.

. . .

This is fiction, not history, so it should not be used as a reference book. I say, for example, that the United States Ambassador to Austria-Hungary at the outbreak of the First World War was Henry Clowes, of Ohio. The actual ambassador at that time was Frederic Courtland Penfield of Connecticut.

I also say that a neutron bomb is a sort of magic wand, which kills people instantly, but which leaves their property unharmed. This is a fantasy borrowed from enthusiasts for a Third World War. A real neutrom bomb, detonated in a populated area, would cause a lot more suffering and destruction than I have described.

I have also misrepresented Creole, just as the viewpoint character, Rudy Waltz, learning that French dialect, might do. I say that it has only one tense—the present. Creole only seems to have that one tense to a beginner, especially if those speaking it to him know that the present tense is the easiest tense for him.

Peace.

—K.V.

Who is Celia? What is she?
That all her swains commend her?

—OTTO WALTZ
(1892–1960)

1

To THE AS-YET-UNBORN, to all innocent wisps of undifferentiated nothingness: Watch out for life.

I have caught life. I have come down with life. I was a wisp of undifferentiated nothingness, and then a little peephole opened quite suddenly. Light and sound poured in. Voices began to describe me and my surroundings. Nothing they said could be appealed. They said I was a boy named Rudolph Waltz, and that was that. They said the year was 1932, and that was that. They said I was in Midland City, Ohio, and that was that.

They never shut up. Year after year they piled detail upon detail. They do it still. You know what they say now? They say the year is 1982, and that I am fifty years old.

Blah blah blah.

• • •

My father was Otto Waltz, whose peephole opened in 1892, and he was told, among other things, that he was the heir to a fortune earned principally by a quack medicine known as "Saint Elmo's Remedy." It was grain alcohol dyed purple, flavored with cloves and sarsaparilla root, and laced with opium and cocaine. As the joke goes: It was absolutely harmless unless discontinued.

He, too, was a Midland City native. He was an only child, and his mother, on the basis of almost no evidence whatsoever, concluded that he could be another Leonardo da Vinci. She had a studio built for him on a loft of the carriage house behind the family mansion when he was only ten years old, and she hired a rapscallion German cabinetmaker, who had studied art in Berlin in his youth, to give Father drawing and painting lessons on weekends and after school.

It was a sweet racket for both teacher and pupil. The teacher's name was August Gunther, and his peephole must have opened in Germany around 1850. Teaching paid as well as cabinetmaking, and, unlike cabinetmaking, allowed him to be as drunk as he pleased.

After Father's voice changed, moreover, Gunther could take him on overnight visits by rail to Indianapolis and Cincinnati and Louisville and Cleveland and so on, ostensibly to visit galleries and painters' studios. The two of them also managed to get drunk, and to become darlings of the fanciest whorehouses in the Middle West.

Was either one of them about to acknowledge that Father couldn't paint or draw for sour apples?

• • •

Who else was there to detect the fraud? Nobody. There wasn't anybody else in Midland City who cared enough about art to notice if Father was gifted or not. He might as well have been a scholar of Sanskrit, as far as the rest of the town was concerned.

Midland City wasn't a Vienna or a Paris. It wasn't even a St. Louis or a Detroit. It was a Bucyrus. It was a Kokomo.

• • •

Gunther's treachery was discovered, but too late. He and Father were arrested in Chicago after doing considerable property damage in a whorehouse there, and Father was found to have gonorrhea, and so on. But Father was by then a fully committed, eighteen-year-old good-time Charley.

Gunther was denounced and fired and blacklisted. Grandfather and Grandmother Waltz were tremendously influential citizens, thanks to Saint Elmo's Remedy. They spread the word that nobody of quality in Midland City was ever to hire Gunther for cabinetwork or any other sort of work—ever again.

Father was sent to relatives in Vienna, to have his gonorrhea treated and to enroll in the world-famous Academy of Fine Arts. While he was on the high seas, in a first-class cabin aboard the *Lusitania,* his parents' mansion burned down. It was widely suspected that the showplace was torched by August Gunther, but no proof was found.

Father's parents, rather than rebuild, took up residence in their thousand-acre farm out near Shepherds-town—leaving behind the carriage house and a cellar hole.

This was in 1910—four years before the outbreak of the First World War.

.   .   .

So Father presented himself at the Academy of Fine Arts with a portfolio of pictures he had created in Midland City. I myself have examined some of the artwork of his youth, which Mother used to moon over after he died. He was good at cross-hatching and shading a drapery, and August Gunther must have been capable in those areas, too. But with few exceptions, everything Father depicted wound up looking as though it were made of cement—a cement woman in a cement dress, walking a cement dog, a herd of cement cattle, a cement bowl of cement fruit, set before a window with cement curtains, and so on.

He was no good at catching likenesses, either. He showed the Academy several portraits of his mother, and I have no idea what she looked like. Her peephole closed long before mine opened. But I do know that no two of Father's portraits of her resemble each other in the least.

Father was told to come back to the Academy in two weeks, at which time they would tell him whether they would take him in or not.

He was in rags at the time, with a piece of rope for a belt, and with patched trousers and so on—although he was receiving an enormous allowance from home. Vienna was then the capital of a great empire, and there were so many elaborate uniforms and exotic costumes, and so much wine and music that it seemed to Father to be a fancy dress ball. So he decided to come to the party as a starving artist. What fun!

And he must have been very good-looking then, for he was, in my opinion, the best-looking man in Midland City when I got to know him a quarter of a century later. He was slender and erect to the end. He was six feet tall. His eyes were blue. He had curly golden hair, and he had lost almost none of it when his peephole closed, when he was allowed to stop being Otto Waltz, when he became just another wisp of undifferentiated nothingness again.

• • •

So he came back in two weeks, and a professor handed him back his portfolio, saying that his work was ludicrous. And there was another young man in rags there, and he, too, had his portfolio returned with scorn.

His name was Adolf Hitler. He was a native Austrian. He had come from Linz.

And Father was so mad at the professor that he got his revenge right then and there. He asked to see some of Hitler's work, with the professor looking on. He picked a picture at random, and he said it was a brilliant piece of work, and he bought it from Hitler for more cash on the spot than the professor, probably, could earn in a month or more.

Only an hour before, Hitler had sold his overcoat so that he could get a little something to eat, even though winter was coming on. So there is a chance that, if it weren't for my father, Hitler might have died of pneumonia or malnutrition in 1910.

Father and Hitler paired off for a while, as people will—comforting and amusing each other, jeering at the art establishment which had rejected them, and so on. I know they took several long walking trips, just the two of them. I learned of their good times together from Mother. When I was old enough to be curious about Father's past, World War Two was about to break out, and Father had developed lockjaw as far as his friendship with Hitler was concerned.

Think of that: My father could have strangled the worst monster of the century, or simply let him starve or freeze to death. But he became his bosom buddy instead.

That is my principal objection to life, I think: It is too easy, when alive, to make perfectly horrible mistakes.

. . .

The painting Father bought from Hitler was a watercolor which is now generally acknowledged as having been the best thing the monster ever did as a painter, and it hung for many years over my parents' bed in Midland City, Ohio. Its title was: "The Minorite Church of Vienna."

2

Father was so well received in Vienna, known to one and all as an American millionaire disguised as a ragged genius, that he roistered there for nearly four years. When the First World War broke out in August of 1914, he imagined that the fancy dress ball was to become a fancy dress picnic, that the party was to be moved out into the countryside. He was so happy, so naive, so self-enchanted, that he asked influential friends if they couldn't get him a commission in the Hungarian Life Guard, whose officers' uniforms included a panther skin.

He adored that panther skin.

He was summoned by the American ambassador to the Austro-Hungarian Empire, Henry Clowes, who was a Cleveland man and an acquaintance of Father's parents. Father was then twenty-two years old. Clowes told Father that he would lose his American citizenship if he joined a foreign army, and that he had made inquiries about Father, and had learned that Father was not the painter he pretended to be, and that Father had been spending money like a drunken sailor, and that he had written to Father's parents, telling them that their son had lost all touch with reality, and that it was time Father was summoned home and given some honest work to do.

"What if I refuse?" said Father.

"Your parents have agreed to stop your allowance," said Clowes.

So Father went home.

• • •

I do not believe he would have stayed in Midland City, if it weren't for what remained of his childhood home, which was its fanciful carriage house. It was hexagonal. It was stone. It had a conical slate roof. It had a naked skeleton inside of noble oak beams. It was a little piece of Europe in southwestern Ohio. It was a present from my great-grandfather Waltz to his homesick wife from Hamburg. It was a stone-by-stone replica of a structure in an illustration in her favorite book of German fairy tales.

It still stands.

I once showed it to an art historian from Ohio University, which is in Athens, Ohio. He said that the original might have been a medieval granary built on the ruins of a Roman watchtower from the time of Julius Caesar. Caesar was murdered two thousand years ago.

Think of that.

• • •

I do not think my father was entirely ungifted as an artist. Like his friend Hitler, he had a flair for romantic architecture. And he set about transforming the carriage house into a painter's studio fit for the reincarnated Leonardo da Vinci his doting mother still believed him to be.

Father's mother was as crazy as a bedbug, my own mother said.

• • •

I sometimes think that I would have had a very different sort of soul, if I had grown up in an ordinary little American house—if our home had not been vast.

Father got rid of all the horse-drawn vehicles in the carriage house—a sleigh, a buckboard, a surrey, a phaeton, a brougham, and who-knows-what-all? Then he had ten horse stalls and a tack room ripped out. This gave him for his private enjoyment more uninterrupted floor-space beneath a far higher ceiling than was afforded by any house of worship or public building in the Midland City of that time.

Was it big enough for a basketball game? A basketball court is ninety-four feet long and fifty feet wide. My childhood home was only eighty feet in diameter. So, no—it lacked fourteen feet of being big enough for a basketball game.

• • •

There were two pairs of enormous doors in the carriage house, wide enough to admit a carriage and a team of horses. One pair faced north, one pair faced south. Father had his workmen take down the northern pair, which his old mentor, August Gunther, made into two tables, a dining table and a table on which Father's paints and brushes and palette knives and charcoal sticks and so on were to be displayed.

The doorway was then filled with what remains the largest window in the city, admitting copious quantities of that balm for all great painters, northern light.

It was before this window that Father's easel stood.

• • •

Yes, he had been reunited with the disreputable August Gunther, who must have been in his middle sixties then. Old Gunther had only one child, a daughter named Grace, so Father was like a son to him. A more suitable son for Gunther would be hard to imagine.

Mother was just a little girl then, and living in a mansion next door. She was terrified of old Gunther. She told me one time that all nice little girls were supposed to run away from him. Right up until the time Mother died, she cringed if August Gunther was mentioned. He was a hobgoblin to her. He was the bogeyman.

As for the pair of great doors facing south: Father had them bolted shut and padlocked, and the workmen caulked the cracks between and around them, to keep out the wind. And then August Gunther cut a front door into one of them. That was the entrance to Father's studio, what would later be my childhood home.

A hexagonal loft encircled and overhung the great chamber. This was partitioned off into bedrooms and bathrooms and a small library.

Above that was an attic under the conical slate roof. Father had no immediate use for the attic, so it was left in its primitive condition.

It was all so impractical—which I guess was the whole idea.

Father was so elated by the vastness of the ground floor, which was paved with cobblestones laid in sand, that he considered putting the kitchen up on a loft. But that would have put the servants and all their hustle and bustle and cooking smells up among the bedrooms. There was no basement to put them in.

So he reluctantly put the kitchen on the ground floor, tucked under a loft and partitioned off with old boards. It was cramped and stuffy. I would love it. I would feel so safe and cozy in there.

• • •

Many people found our house spooky, and the attic in fact was full of evil when I was born. It housed a collection of more than three hundred antique and modern firearms. Father had bought them during his and Mother's six-month honeymoon in Europe in 1922. Father thought them beautiful, but they might as well have been copperheads and rattlesnakes.

They were murder.

3

My mother's peephole opened in Midland City in 1901. She was nine years younger than Father. She, like him, was an only child—the daughter of Richard Wetzel, the founder and principal stockholder of the Midland County National Bank. Her name was Emma.

She was born into a mansion teeming with servants, right next door to my father's childhood home, but she would die penniless in 1978, four years ago now, in a little shitbox she and I shared in the suburb of Midland City called Avondale.

. . .

She remembered seeing Father's childhood home burn down when she was nine years old, when Father was on his way to Vienna. But Father made a far greater impression on her than the fire when he came home from Vienna and looked over the carriage house with the idea of turning it into a studio.

She had her first glimpse of him through the privet

hedge between the two properties. This was a bird-legged, buck-toothed, skinny thirteen-year-old, who had never seen men dressed in anything but overalls or business suits. Her parents had spoken glowingly of Father, since he was rich and came from an excellent family. They had suggested playfully that she could do worse than marry him someday.

So now she peeked at him through the hedge, her heart beating madly, and, great God! He was all scarlet and silver, except for a panther skin over one shoulder—and a sable busby with a purple plume on his head.

He was wearing one of the many souvenirs he had brought home from Vienna, which was the dress uniform of a major in the Hungarian Life Guard, the regiment he had hoped to join.

• • •

A real Hungarian Life Guard back in the Austro-Hungarian Empire might have been putting on a field gray uniform about then.

Father's friend Hitler, who was an Austrian, had managed to join the German rather than the Austrian army—because he admired all things German so much. He was wearing field gray.

• • •

Father was living with his parents out near Shepherdstown at the time, but all his souvenirs were stored in the carriage house. And, on the day that Mother saw him in the uniform, he had begun opening trunks and packing cases, with his old mentor, August Gunther, looking on. He had put on the uniform to make Gunther laugh.

They came outside, lugging a table between them. They were going to have lunch in the shade of an ancient walnut tree. They had brought beer and bread and sausage and cheese and roast chicken, all of which had been produced locally. The cheese, incidentally, was Liederkranz, which most people assume is a European cheese. Liederkranz was invented in Midland City, Ohio, in about 1865.

• • •

So Father, setting down for a lusty lunch with old Gunther, was aware that a little girl was watching everything through the hedge, and he made jokes about her which she could hear. He said to Gunther that he had been away so long that he could no longer remember the names of American birds. There was a bird in the hedge there, he said, and he described Mother as though she were a bird, and he asked old Gunther what to call the bird.

And Father approached the supposed little bird with a piece of bread in his hand, asking if little birds like her ate bread, and Mother fled into her parents' house.

She told me this. Father told me this.

• • •

But she came out again, and she found a better place to spy from—where she could see without being seen. There were puzzling new arrivals at the picnic. They were two short, dark youths, who had evidently been wading. They were barefoot, and their trousers were wet above the knees. Mother had never seen anything quite like them for this reason: The two, who were brothers, were Italians, and there had never been Italians in Midland City before.

They were Gino Maritimo, eighteen, and Marco Maritimo, twenty. They were in one hell of a lot of trouble. They weren't expected at the picnic. They weren't even supposed to be in the United States. Thirty-six hours before, they had been stokers aboard an Italian freighter which was taking on cargo in Newport News, Virginia. They had jumped ship in order to escape military conscription at home, and because the streets of America were paved with gold. They spoke no English.

Other Italians in Newport News boosted them and their cardboard suitcases into an empty boxcar in a train that was bound for God-knows-where. The train began to move immediately. The sun went down. There were no stars, no moon that night. America was blackness and *clackety-clack*.

How do I know what the night was like? Gino and Marco Maritimo, as old men, both told me so.

• • •

Somewhere in the seamless darkness, which may have been West Virginia, Gino and Marco were joined by four American hoboes, who at knife-point took their suitcases, their coats, their hats, and their shoes.

They were lucky they didn't have their throats slit for fun. Who would have cared?

• • •

How they wished that their peepholes would close! But the nightmare went on and on. And then it became a daymare. The train stopped several times, but in the midst of such ugliness that Gino and Marco could not bring themselves to step out into it, to somehow start living there. But then two railroad detectives with long clubs made them get out anyway, and, like it or lump it, they were on the outskirts of Midland City, Ohio, on the other side of Sugar Creek from the center of town.

They were terribly hungry and thirsty. They could either await death, or they could invent something to do. They invented. They saw a conical slate roof on the other side of the river, and they walked toward that. In order to keep putting one foot in front of the other, they pretended that it was of utmost importance that they reach that structure and no other.

They waded across Sugar Creek, rather than draw attention to themselves on the bridge. They would have swum the creek, if it had been that deep.

And now here they were, as astonished as my mother had been to see a young man all dressed in scarlet and silver, with a sable busby on his head.

When Father looked askance at the two of them from his seat under the oak, Gino, the younger of the brothers, but their leader, said in Italian that they were hungry and would do any sort of work for food.

Father replied in Italian. He was good with languages. He was fluent in French and German and Spanish, too. He told the brothers that they should by all means sit down and eat, if they were as hungry as they appeared to be. He said that nobody should ever be hungry.

He was like a god to them. It was so easy for him to be like a god to them.

After they had eaten, he took them up into the attic above the loft, the future gun room. There were two old cots up there. Light and air came from windows in a cupola at the peak of the roof. A ladder, its bottom bolted to the center of the attic floor, led up into the cupola. Father told the brothers that they could make the attic their home, until they found something better.

He said he had some old shoes and sweaters and so on, if they wanted them, in his trunks below.

He put them to work the next day, ripping out the stalls and tack room.

And no matter how rich and powerful the Maritimo brothers subsequently became, and no matter how disreputable and poor Father became, Father remained a god to them.

4

And somewhere in there, before America entered the First World War against the German Empire and the Austro-Hungarian Empire and the Ottoman Empire, Father's parents had their peepholes closed by carbon monoxide from a faulty heating system in their farmhouse out near Shepherdstown.

So Father became a major stockholder in the family business, the Waltz Brothers Drug Company, to which he had contributed nothing but ridicule and scorn.

And he attended stockholders' meetings in a beret and a paint-stained smock and sandals, and he brought old August Gunther along, claiming Gunther was his lawyer, and he protested that he found his two uncles and their several sons, who actually ran the business, intolerably humorless and provincial and obsessed by profits, and so on.

He would ask them when they were going to stop poisoning their fellow citizens, and so on. At that time, the uncles and cousins were starting the first chain of drugstores in the history of the country, and they were especially proud of the soda fountains in those stores, and had spent a lot of money to guarantee that the ice cream served at those fountains was the equal of any ice cream in the world. So Father wanted to know why ice cream at a Waltz Brothers Drugstore always tasted like library paste, and so on.

He was an artist, you see, interested in enterprises far loftier than mere pharmacy.

And now is perhaps the time for me to name my own profession. Guess what? I, Rudy Waltz, the son of that great artist Otto Waltz, am a registered pharmacist.

• • •

Somewhere in there, one end of a noble oak timber was dropped on Father's left foot. Alcohol was involved in the accident. During a wild party at the studio, with tools and building materials lying all around, Father got a structural idea which had to be carried out at once. Nothing would do but that the drunken guests become common laborers under Father's command, and a young dairy farmer named John Fortune lost his grip on a timber. It fell on Father's foot, smashing the bones of his instep. Two of his toes died, and had to be cut away.

Thus was Father rendered unfit for military service when America got into World War One.

• • •

Father once said to me when he was an old man, after he had spent two years in prison, after he and Mother had lost all their money and art treasures in a lawsuit, that his greatest disappointment in life was that he had never been a soldier. That was almost the last illusion he had, and there might have been some substance to it—that he had been born to serve bravely and resourcefully on a battlefield.

He certainly envied John Fortune to the end. The man who crushed his foot went on to become a hero in the trenches in the First World War, and Father would have liked to have fought beside him—and, like Fortune, come home with medals on his chest. The only remotely military honor Father would ever receive was a citation from the governor of Ohio for Father's leadership of scrap drives in Midland County during World War Two. There was no ceremony. The certificate simply arrived in the mail one day.

Father was in prison over at Shepherdstown when it came. Mother and I brought it to him on visitors' day. I was thirteen then. It would have been kinder of us to burn it up and scatter its ashes over Sugar Creek. That certificate was the crowning irony, as far as Father was concerned.

"At last I have joined the company of the immortals," he said. "There are only two more honors for me to covet now." One was to be a licensed dog. The other was to be a notary public.

And Father made us hand over the certificate so that he could wipe his behind with it at the earliest opportunity, which he surely did.

Instead of saying good-bye that day, he said this, a finger in the air: "Nature calls."

• • •

And somewhere in there, in the autumn of 1916, to be exact, the old rascal August Gunther died under most mysterious circumstances. He got up two hours before dawn one day, and prepared and ate a hearty breakfast while his wife and daughter slept. And he set out on foot, armed with a double-barreled ten-gauge shotgun which my father had given to him, meaning to join Father and John Fortune and some other young bucks in gun pits on the edge of a meadow on John Fortune's father's dairy farm. They were going to shoot geese which had spent the night on the backwaters of Sugar Creek and on Crystal Lake. The meadow had been baited with cracked corn.

He never reached the gun pits, or so the story went. So he must have died somewhere in the intervening five miles, which included the Sugar Creek Bridge. One month later, his headless body was found at the mouth of Sugar Creek just west of Cincinnati, about to start its voyage to the Mississippi and the Gulf of Mexico and beyond.

What a vacation from Midland City!

And when I was little, the decapitation of August Gunther so long ago, sixteen years before my birth, was the most legendary of all the unsolved crimes committed in my hometown. And I had a ghoulish ambition. I imagined that I would be famous and admired, if only I could find August Gunther's missing head. And after that the murderer would have to confess, for some reason, and he would be taken off to be punished, and so on—and the mayor would pin a medal on me.

Little did I suspect back then that I myself, Rudy Waltz, would become a notorious murderer known as "Deadeye Dick."

. . .

My parents were married in 1922, four years after the end of the First World War. Father was thirty and Mother was twenty-one. Mother was a college graduate, having taken a liberal arts degree at Oberlin College in Oberlin, Ohio. Father, who certainly encouraged people to believe that he had spent time at some great and ancient European university, was in fact only a high school graduate. He could certainly lecture on history or race or biology or art or politics for hours, although he had read very little.

Almost all his opinions and information were cannibalized from the educations and miseducations of his roistering companions in Vienna before the First World War.

And one of these pals was Hitler, of course.

. . .

The wedding and the reception took place in the Wetzel mansion, next door to the studio. The Wetzels and the Waltzes were proudly agnostic, so the ceremony was performed by a judge. Father's best man was John Fortune, the war hero and dairy farmer. Mother's attendants were friends from Oberlin.

Father's immediate relatives, the uncles and cousins who earned his living for him, came with their mates to the wedding, but they stayed for only a few minutes of the reception, behaving correctly but coldly, and then they departed en masse. Father had given them every reason to loathe him.

Father laughed. According to Mother, he announced to the rest of the guests that he was sorry, but that his relatives had to go back to the countinghouse.

He was quite the bohemian!

· · ·

So then he and Mother went on a six-month honeymoon in Europe. While they were away, the Waltz Brothers Drug Company was moved to Chicago, where it already had a cosmetics factory and three drugstores.

When Mother and Father came home, they were the only Waltzes in town.

· · ·

It was during the honeymoon that Father acquired his famous gun collection, or most of it—at a single whack. He and Mother visited what was left of the family of a friend from the good old days in Vienna, Rudolf von Furstenberg, outside of Salzburg, Austria. Rudolf had been killed in the war, and so had his father and two brothers, and I am named after him. His mother and his youngest brother survived, but they were bankrupt. Everything on the estate was for sale.

So Father bought the collection of more than three hundred guns, which encompassed almost the entire history of firearms up until 1914 or so. Several of the weapons were American, including a Colt .45 revolver and a .30-06 Springfield rifle. As powerful as those two guns were, Father taught me how to fire them and handle their violent kicks, and to clean them, and to take them apart and put them back together again while blindfolded, when I was only ten years old.

God bless him.

• • •

And Mother and Father bought a lot of the von Furstenbergs' furniture and linens and crystal, and some battle-axes and swords, chain maces, and helmets and shields.

My brother and I were both conceived in a von Furstenberg bed, with a coat of arms on the headboard, and with "The Minorite Church of Vienna," by Adolf Hitler, on the wall over that.

• • •

Mother and Father went looking for Hitler, too, on their honeymoon. But he was in jail.

He had risen to the rank of corporal in the war, and had won an Iron Cross for delivering messages under fire. So Father had close friends who had been heroes on both sides of the war.

• • •

Father and Mother also bought the enormous weather vane from the gatehouse of the von Furstenberg estate, and put it atop their cupola back home, making the studio taller than anything in the county, except for the dome of the county courthouse, a few silos, the Fortunes' dairy barn, and the Midland County National Bank.

That weather vane was instantly the most famous work of art in Midland City. Its only competition was a statue of a Union soldier on foot in Fairchild Park. Its arrow alone was twelve feet long, and one hollow copper horseman chased another one down that awesome shaft. The one in back was an Austrian with a lance. The one in front, fleeing for his life, was a Turk with a scimitar.

This engine, swinging now toward Detroit, now toward Louisville, and so on, commemorated the lifting of the Turkish siege of Vienna in 1683.

When I was little, I asked my brother Felix, who is seven years older than I am, and who used to lie to me every chance he got, to explain to me and a playmate the significance of the weather vane. He was in high school then. He already had the beautiful, deep purple voice which would prove to be his fortune in the communications industry.

"If the Austrians hadn't won," he said in a solemn rumble, "Mother would be in a harem now. Father would be passing out towels in a steam bath, and you and I and your friend here would probably have our balls cut off."

I believed him at the time.

5

ADOLF HITLER became chancellor of Germany in 1933, when I was one year old. Father, who had not seen him since 1914, sent his heartiest congratulations and a gift, Hitler's watercolor, "The Minorite Church of Vienna."

Hitler was charmed. He had fond memories of Father, he said, and he invited him to come to Germany as his personal guest, to see the new social order he was building, which he expected to last a thousand years or more.

Mother and Father and Felix, who was then nine, went to Germany for six months in 1934, leaving me behind and in the care of servants, all black people. Why should I have gone? I was only two. It was surely then that I formed the opinion that the servants were my closest relatives. I aspired to do what they did so well—to cook and bake and wash dishes, and to make the beds and wash and iron and spade the garden, and so on.

It still makes me as happy as I can be to prepare a

good meal in a house which, because of me, is sparkling clean.

. . .

I have no conscious memory of what my real relatives looked like when they came home from Germany. Perhaps a hypnotist could help me come up with one. But I have since seen photographs of them—in a scrapbook Mother kept of those exciting days, and also in old copies of the *Midland City Bugle-Observer*. Mother is wearing a dirndl. Father is wearing lederhosen and knee socks. Felix, although technically not entitled to do so, since he never joined the organization, was wearing the khaki uniform and Sam Browne belt, and the armband with swastika and ornamental dagger of the Hitler Youth. Even if Felix had been a German boy, he would have been too young to wear an outfit like that, but Father had a tailor in Berlin make it up for him anyway.

Why not?

. . .

And as soon as those relatives of mine got home, according to the paper, Father flew his favorite gift from Hitler from the horizontal shaft of the weather vane. It was a Nazi flag as big as a bedsheet.

Again: This was only 1934, and World War Two was still a long way off. It was a long way off, that is, if five years can be considered a long way off. So flying a Nazi flag in Midland City was no more offensive than flying a Greek or

Irish or Confederate flag, or whatever. It was a playful, exuberant thing to do, and, according to Mother, the community was proud and envious of Father and her and Felix. Nobody else in Midland City was friendly with a head of state.

I myself am in one picture in the paper. It is of our entire family in the street in front of the studio, looking up at the Nazi flag. I am in the arms of Mary Hoobler, our cook. She would teach me everything she knew about cooking and baking, by and by.

• • •

Mary Hoobler's corn bread: Mix together in a bowl half a cup of flour, one and a half cups of yellow cornmeal, a teaspoon of salt, a teaspoon of sugar, and three teaspoons of baking powder. Add three beaten eggs, a cup of milk, a half cup of cream, and a half cup of melted butter.

Pour it into a well-buttered pan and bake it at four hundred degrees for fifteen minutes.

Cut it into squares while it is still hot. Bring the squares to the table while they are still hot, and folded in a napkin.

• • •

When we all posed in the street for our picture in the paper, Father was forty-two. According to Mother, he had undergone a profound spiritual change in Germany. He had a new sense of purpose in life. It was no longer enough to be an artist. He would become a teacher and political activist. He would become a spokesman in America for the new social order which was being born in Germany, but which in time would be the salvation of the world.

This was quite a mistake.

• • •

How to make Mary Hoobler's barbecue sauce: Sauté a cup of chopped onions and three chopped garlic cloves in a quarter of a pound of butter until tender. Add a half cup of catsup, a quarter cup of brown sugar, a teaspoon of salt, two teaspoons of freshly ground pepper, a dash of Tabasco, a tablespoon of lemon juice, a teaspoon of basil, and a tablespoon of chili powder.

Bring to a boil and simmer for five minutes.

• • •

So for two years and a little bit more, Father lectured and showed films and lantern slides of the new Germany all over the Middle West. He told heartwarming stories about his friend Hitler, and explained Hitler's theories about the variously superior and inferior human races as being simple chemistry. A pure Jew was this. A pure German was that. Cross a Pole with a Negro, you were certain to get an amusing laborer.

It must have been terrible.

I remember the Nazi flag hanging on the wall of our living room—or I think I do. I certainly heard about it. It used to be the first thing that visitors saw when they came in. It was so colorful. Everything else was so dull by comparison—the timbers and stone walls, the great tables made of carriage-house doors; Father's rustic easel, which looked like a guillotine, silhouetted against the north window; the medieval weapons and armor rusting here and there.

• • •

I close my eyes and I try to see the flag in my memory. I can't. I shiver, though—because our house, except for the kitchen, was always so cold in the wintertime.

• • •

That house was a perfect son of a bitch to heat. Father wanted to see the bare stones of the walls, and the bare boards that supported the slate roof over the gun room.

Even at the end of his life, when my brother Felix was paying the heating bill, Father would not hear of insulation.

"After I am dead," he said.

• • •

Mother and Father and Felix never used to complain about the cold. They wore lots of clothes in the house, and said everybody else's house in America was too warm, and that all that heat slowed the blood and made people lazy and stupid and so on.

That, too, must have been part of the Nazi thing.

They would make me come out of the little kitchen and into the vast draftiness of the rest of the ground floor, so that I would grow up hardy and vigorous, I suppose. But I was soon back in the kitchen again, where it was so hot and fragrant. It was comical in there, too, since it was the only room in the house where any meaningful work was going on, and yet it was as cramped as a ship's galley. The people who did nothing, who were merely waited on, had all the space.

And on cold days, and even on days that weren't all that cold, the rest of the servants, the yardman and the upstairs maid and so on, all black, would crowd into the kitchen with the cook and me. They liked being crowded together. When they were little, they told me, they slept in beds with a whole lot of brothers and sisters. That sounded like a lot of fun to me. It still sounds like a lot of fun to me.

There in the crowded kitchen, everybody would talk and talk and talk so easily, just blather and blather and laugh and laugh. I was included in the conversation. I was a nice little boy. Everybody liked me.

"What you got to say about that, Mister Rudy?" a servant would ask me, and I would say something, anything, and everybody would pretend I had said something wise or intentionally funny.

If I had died in childhood, I would have thought life was that little kitchen. I would have done anything to get back into that kitchen again—on the coldest day in the wintertime.

Carry me back to old Virginny.

• • •

Somewhere in there the Nazi flag came down. Father stopped traveling. According to my brother Felix, who was an eighth-grader at the time, Father wouldn't even leave the house or talk on the telephone, or look at his mail for three months or more. He went into such a deep depression that it was feared that he might commit suicide, so that Mother took the gun-room key from his key ring. He never missed it. He had no inclination to visit his beloved firearms.

Felix says that Father might have crashed like that, no matter what was really going on in the outside world. But the mail and telephone calls he was receiving were getting meaner all the time, and G-men had visited him, and suggested that he register as an agent for a foreign power, in order to comply with the law of the land. The man who had been his best man at his wedding, John Fortune, had stopped speaking to him, and had been going around town, to Father's certain knowledge, declaring Father to be a dangerous nincompoop.

Which Father surely was.

Fortune himself was of totally Germanic extraction. His last name was simply an Anglicization of the German word for luck, which is *Glück*.

Fortune would never give Father an opportunity to mend the rupture between them, for, in 1938, he suddenly took off for the Himalayas, in search of far higher happiness and wisdom than was available, evidently, in Midland City,

Ohio. His wife had died of cancer. He was childless. There had been some defect in his or his wife's reproductive apparatus. The family dairy farm went bankrupt, and was taken over by the Midland County National Bank.

And John Fortune is buried now in bib overalls—in the capital city of Nepal, which is Katmandu.

6

M IDLAND CITY has now been depopulated by a
neutron bomb explosion. It was a big news story for about
ten days or so. It might have been a bigger story, a signal
for the start of World War Three, if the Government hadn't
acknowledged at once that the bomb was made in America. One newscast I heard down here in Haiti called it "a
friendly bomb."

The official story is that an American truck was trans-
porting this American bomb on the Interstate, and the
bomb went off. There was this flash. It was an accident,
supposedly. The truck, if there really was a truck, seems
to have been right opposite the new Holiday Inn and
Dwayne Hoover's Exit 11 Pontiac Village when the bomb
went off.

Everybody in the county was killed, including five
people awaiting execution on death row in the Adult Cor-
rectional Institution at Shepherdstown. I certainly lost a lot
of acquaintances all at once.

But most of the structures are still left standing and furnished. I am told that every one of the television sets in the new Holiday Inn is still fully operable. So are all the telephones. So is the ice-cube maker behind the bar. All those sensitive devices were only a few hundred yards from the source of the flash.

So nobody lives in Midland City, Ohio, anymore. About one hundred thousand people died. That was roughly the population of Athens during the Golden Age of Pericles. That is two-thirds of the population of Katmandu.

And I do not see how I can get out of asking this question: Does it matter to anyone or anything that all those peepholes were closed so suddenly? Since all the property is undamaged, has the world lost anything it loved?

• • •

Midland City isn't radioactive. New people could move right in. There is talk now of turning it over to Haitian refugees.

Good luck to them.

• • •

There is an arts center there. If the neutrons were going to knock over anything, you might think, it would have been the Mildred Barry Center for the Arts, since it looks so frail and exposed—a white sphere on four slender stilts in the middle of Sugar Creek.

It has never been used. The walls of its galleries are bare. What a delightful opportunity it would represent to Haitians, who are the most prolific painters and sculptors in the history of the world.

The most gifted Haitian could refurbish my father's studio. It is time a real artist lived there—with all that north light flooding in.

• • •

Haitians speak Creole, a French dialect which has only a present tense. I have lived in Haiti with my brother for the past six months, so I can speak it some. Felix and I are innkeepers now. We have bought the Grand Hotel Oloffson, a gingerbread palace at the base of a cliff in Port au Prince.

Imagine a language with only a present tense. Our headwaiter, Hippolyte Paul De Mille, who claims to be eighty and have fifty-nine descendants, asked me about my father.

"He is dead?" he said in Creole.

"He is dead," I agreed. There could be no argument about that.

"What does he do?" he said.

"He paints," I said.

"I like him," he said.

• • •

Haitian fresh fish in coconut cream: Put two cups of grated coconut in cheesecloth over a bowl. Pour a cup of hot milk over it, and squeeze it dry. Repeat this with two more cups of hot milk. The stuff in the bowl is the sauce.

Mix a pound of sliced onions, a teaspoon of salt, a half teaspoon of black pepper, and a teaspoon of crushed pepper. Sauté the mixture in butter until soft but not brown. Add four pounds of fresh fish chunks, and cook them for about a minute on each side.

Pour the sauce over the fish, cover the pan, and simmer for ten minutes. Uncover the pan and baste the fish until it is done—and the sauce has become creamy.

Serves eight vaguely disgruntled guests at the Grand Hotel Oloffson.

• • •

Imagine a language with only a present tense. Or imagine my father, who was wholly a creature of the past. To all practical purposes, he spent most of his adult life, except for the last fifteen years, at a table in a Viennese café before the First World War. He was forever twenty years old or so. He would paint wonderful pictures by and by. He would be a devil-may-care soldier by and by. He was already a lover and a philosopher and a nobleman.

I don't think he even noticed Midland City before I became a murderer. It was as though he were in a space suit, with the atmosphere of prewar Vienna inside. He used to speak so inappropriately to my playmates, and to Felix's friends, whenever we were foolish enough to bring them home.

At least I didn't go through what Felix went through when he was in junior high school. Back then, Father used to say "Heil Hitler" to Felix's guests, and they were expected to say "Heil Hitler" back, and it was all supposed to be such lusty fun.

"My God," Felix said only the other afternoon, "—it was bad enough that we were the richest kids in town, and everybody else was having such a hard time, and there was all this rusty medieval shit hanging on the walls, as though it were a torture chamber. Couldn't we at least have had a father who didn't say 'Heil Hitler,' to everyone, including Izzy Finkelstein?"

• • •

About how much money we had, even though the Great Depression was going on: Father sold off all his Waltz Brothers Drug Company stock in the 1920s, so when the chain fell apart during the Depression, it meant nothing to him. He bought Coca-Cola stock, which acted the way he did, as though it didn't even know a depression was going on. And Mother still had all the bank stock she had inherited from her father. Because of all the prime farmland it had acquired through foreclosures, it was as good as gold.

This was dumb luck.

• • •

It was soda fountains as much as the Depression that wrecked the Waltz Brothers chain. Pharmacists have no business being in the food business, too. Leave the food business to those who know and love it.

One of Father's favorite jokes, I remember, was about the boy who flunked out of pharmacy school. He didn't know how to make a club sandwich.

• • •

There is still one Waltz Brothers Drugstore left, I have heard, in Cairo, Illinois. It certainly has nothing to do with me, or with any of my relatives, wherever they may be. I gather that it is part of a cute, old-fashioned urban renewal scheme in downtown Cairo. The streets are cobblestoned, like the floor of my childhood home. The streetlights are gas.

And there is an old-fashioned pool hall and an old-fashioned saloon and an old-fashioned firehouse and an old-fashioned drugstore with a soda fountain. Somebody found an old sign from a Waltz Brothers drugstore, and they hung it up again.

It was so quaint.

I hear they have a poster inside, too, which sings the praises of Saint Elmo's Remedy.

They wouldn't dare really stock Saint Elmo's Remedy today, of course, it was so bad for people. The poster is just a joke. But they have a modern prescription counter, where you can get barbiturates and amphetamines and methaqualones and so on.

Science marches on.

• • •

By the time I was old enough to bring guests home, Father had stopped mentioning Hitler to anyone. That much about the present had got through to him, anyway: The subject of Hitler and the new order in Germany seemed to make people angrier with each passing day, so he had better find something else to talk about.

And I do not mean to mock him. He had been just another wisp of undifferentiated nothingness, like the rest of us, and then all the light and sound poured in.

But he assumed that my playmates were thoroughly familiar with Greek mythology and legends of King Arthur's Round Table and the plays of Shakespeare and Cervantes' *Don Quixote,* Goethe's *Faust* and Wagnerian opera and on and on—all of which were no doubt lively subjects in Viennese cafés before the First World War.

So he might say to the eight-year-old son of a toolchecker over at Green Diamond Plow, "You look at me as though I were Mephistopheles. Is that who you think I am? Eh? Eh?"

My guest was expected to answer.

Or he might say to a daughter of a janitor over at the YMCA, offering her a chair, "Do sit down in the Siege Perilous, my dear. Or do you dare?"

Almost all my playmates were children of uneducated parents in humble jobs, since the neighborhood had gone downhill fast after all the rich people but Father and Mother moved away.

Father might say to another one, "I am Daedalus! Would you like me to give you wings so you can fly with me? We can join the geese and fly south with them! But we mustn't fly too close to the sun, must we. Why mustn't we fly too close to the sun, eh? Eh?"

And the child was expected to answer.

On his deathbed at the County Hospital, when Father was listing all his virtues and vices, he said that at least he had been wonderful with children, that they had all found him a lot of fun. "I understand them," he said.

• • •

He gave his most dumbfoundingly inappropriate greeting, however, not to a child but to a young woman named Celia Hildreth. She was a high school senior, as was my brother—and Felix had invited her to the senior prom. This would have been in the springtime of 1943, almost exactly a year before I became a murderer—a double murderer, actually. World War Two was going on.

Felix was the president of his class—because of that deep voice of his. God spoke through him—about where the senior prom should be held, and whether people should have their nicknames under their pictures in the yearbook, and on and on. And he was in the midst of an erotic catastrophe, to which he had made me privy, although I was only eleven years old. Irreconcilable differences had arisen between him and his sweetheart for the past semester and a half, Sally Freeman, and Sally had turned to Steve Adams, the captain of the basketball team, for consolation.

This left the president of the class without a date for the prom, and at a time when every girl of any social importance had been spoken for.

Felix executed a sociological master stroke. He invited a girl who was at the bottom of the social order, whose parents were illiterate and unemployed, who had two brothers in prison, who got very poor grades and engaged in no extracurricular activities, but who, nonetheless, was one of the prettiest young women anybody had ever seen.

Her family was white, but they were so poor that they lived in the black part of town. Also: the few young men who had tried to trifle with her, despite her social class, had spread the word that, no matter what she looked like, she was as cold as ice.

This was Celia Hildreth.

So she could have had scant expectation of being invited to the senior prom. But miracles do happen. A new Cinderella is born every minute. One of the richest, cutest boys in town, and the president of the senior class, no less, invited her to the senior prom.

• • •

So, a few weeks in advance of the prom, Felix talked a lot about how beautiful Celia Hildreth was, and what an impression he was going to make when he appeared with a movie star on his arm. Everybody else there was supposed to feel like a fool for having ignored Celia for so long.

And Father heard all this, and nothing would do but that Felix bring Celia by the studio, on the way to the prom, so that Father, an artist after all, could see for himself if Celia was as beautiful as Felix said. Felix and I had by then given up bringing home friends for any reason whatsoever. But in this instance Father had a means for compelling Felix to introduce him to Celia. If Felix wouldn't do that, then Felix couldn't use the car that night. He and Celia would have to ride a bus to the senior prom.

• • •

Haitian banana soup: Stew two pounds of goat or chicken with a half cup of chopped onions, a teaspoon of salt, half a teaspoon of black pepper, and a pinch of crushed red pepper. Use two quarts of water. Stew for an hour.

Add three peeled yams and three peeled bananas, cut into chunks. Simmer until the meat is tender. Take out the meat.

What is left is eight servings of Haitian banana soup. *Bon appétit!*

• • •

So Father, without enough to do, as usual, was as excited by the approach of prom night as the most bubble-headed senior. He would say over and over:

"Who is Celia? What is she?
That all her swains commend her?"

Or he would protest in the middle of a silence at supper, "She can't be that beautiful! No girl could be that beautiful."

It was to no avail for Felix to tell him that Celia was no world's champion of feminine pulchritude. Felix said many times, "She's just the prettiest girl in the senior class, Dad," but Father imagined a grander adversary. He, the highest judge of beauty in the city, and Celia, one of the most beautiful women ever to live, supposedly, were about to meet eye-to-eye.

Oh, he was leading scrap drives in those days, and he was an air-raid warden, too. And he had helped the War Department to draw up a personality profile of Hitler, who he now said was a brilliant homicidal maniac. But he still felt drab and superannuated and so on, with so many battle reports in the paper and on the radio, and with so many uniforms around. His spirits needed a boost in the very worst way.

And he had a secret. If Felix had guessed it, Felix wouldn't have brought Celia within a mile of home. He would have taken her to the prom on a bus.

This was it: When Celia was introduced to Father, he would be wearing the scarlet-and-silver uniform of a major in the Hungarian Life Guard, complete with sable busby and panther skin.

7

LISTEN: When Felix was ready to fetch Celia, Father wasn't even in his painter's costume. He was wearing a sweater and slacks, and he promised Felix yet again that he simply wanted to catch a glimpse of this girl, and that he wasn't going to put on any kind of a show for her. It was all going to be very ordinary and brief, and even boring.

About the automobile: It was a Keedsler touring car, manufactured right in Midland City in 1932, when a Keedsler was in every respect the equal or the superior of a German Mercedes or a British Rolls-Royce. It was a bizarre and glorious antique even in 1943. Felix had put the top down. There was a separate windshield for the back seat. The engine had sixteen cylinders, and the two spare tires were mounted in shallow wells in the front fenders. The tires looked like the necks of plunging horses.

So Felix burbled off toward the black part of town in that flabbergasting apparatus. He was wearing a rented tuxedo, with a gardenia in his lapel. There was a corsage of two orchids for Celia on the seat beside him.

Father stripped down to his underwear, and Mother brought him the uniform. She was in on this double cross of Felix. She thought everything Father did was wonderful. And while Father was getting dressed again, she went around turning off electric lights and lighting candles. She and Father, without anybody's much noticing it, had earlier in the day put candles everywhere. There must have been a hundred of them.

Mother got them all lit, just about the time Father topped off his scarlet-and-silver uniform with the busby.

And I myself, standing on the balcony outside my bedroom on the loft, was as enchanted as Mother and Father expected Celia Hildreth to be. I was inside a great beehive filled with fireflies. And below me was the beautiful King of the Early Evening.

My mind had been trained by heirloom books of fairy tales, and by the myths and legends which animated my father's conversation, to think that way. It was second nature for me, and for Felix, too, and for no other children in Midland City, I am sure, to see candle flames as fireflies—and to invent a King of the Early Evening.

And now the King of the Early Evening, with a purple plume in his busby, gave this order: "Ope, ope the portals!"

• • •

What portals were there to open? There were only two, I thought. There was the front door on the south, and there was the kitchen door on the northeast. But Father seemed to be calling for something far more majestic than opening both of those.

And then he advanced on the two huge carriage-house doors, in one of which our front door was set. I had never thought of them as doors. They were a wall of my home which was made of wood rather than stone. Now Father took hold of the mighty bolt which had held them shut for thirty years. It resisted him for only a moment, and then slid back, as it had been born to do.

Until that moment, I had seen that bolt as just another dead piece of medieval iron on the wall. In the proper hands, perhaps it could have killed an enemy.

I had felt the same way about the ornate hinges. But they weren't more junk from Europe. They were real Midland City, Ohio, hinges, ready to work at any time.

I had stolen downstairs now, awe in every step I took.

The King of the Early Evening put his shoulder to one carriage-house door and then the other. A wall of my home vanished. There were stars and a rising moon where it had been.

8

And Mother and Father and I all hid as Felix arrived with Celia Hildreth in the Keedsler touring car. Felix, too, was dazed by the lovely transformation of our home. When he switched off the Keedsler's idling engine, it was as though it went on idling anyway. In a voice just like the engine's, he was reassuring Celia that she needn't be afraid, even though she had never seen anything like this house before.

I heard her say this: "I'm sorry. I can't help being scared. I want to get out of here." I was just inside the great new doorway.

That should have been enough for Felix. He should have gotten her out of there. As she would say in a few minutes, she hadn't even wanted to go to the prom, but her parents had told her she had to, and she hated her dress and was ashamed to have anybody see her in it, and she didn't understand rich people, and didn't want to, and she was happiest when she was all alone and nobody could stare at her, and nobody could say things to her that she was supposed to reply to in some fancy, ladylike way—and so on.

Felix used to say that he didn't get her out of there because he wanted to show Father that he could keep a promise, even if Father couldn't. He admits now, though, that he forgot her entirely. He got out of the car, but he didn't go to Celia's side, to open her door for her and offer his arm.

All alone, he walked to the center of the great new doorway, and he stopped there, and he put his hands on his hips, and he looked all around at the galaxy of tiny conflagrations.

He should have been angry, and he would get angry later. He would be like a dog with rabies later on. But, at that moment, he could only acknowledge that his father, after years of embarrassing enthusiasms and ornate irrelevancies, had produced an artistic masterpiece.

Never before had there been such beauty in Midland City.

• • •

And then Father stepped out from behind a vertical timber, the very one which had mashed his left foot so long ago. He was only a yard or two from Felix, and he held an apple in his hand. Celia could see him through the windshield of the Keedsler. He called out, with our house as an echo chamber, "Let Helen of Troy come forward—to claim this apple, if she dare!"

Celia stayed right where she was. She was petrified.

And Felix, having allowed things to go this far, was fool enough to think that maybe she could get out of the car and accept the apple, even though there was no way she could have any idea what was going on.

What did she know of Helen of Troy and apples? For that matter, what did Father know? He had the legend all garbled, as I now realize. Nobody ever gave Helen of Troy an apple—not as a prize, anyway.

It was the goddess Aphrodite who was given a golden apple in the legend—as a prize for being the most beautiful of all the goddesses. A young prince, named Paris, a mortal, chose her over the other two finalists in the contest—Athena and Hera.

So, as though it would have made the least bit of difference on that spring night in 1943, Father should have said, "Let Aphrodite come forward—to claim this apple, if she dare!"

It would have been better still, of course, if he had had himself bound and gagged in the gun room on the night of the senior prom.

As for Helen of Troy, and how she fitted into the legend, not that Celia Hildreth had ever heard of her: She was the most beautiful mortal woman on earth, and Aphrodite donated her to Paris in exchange for the apple.

There was just one trouble with Helen. She was already married to the king of Sparta, so that Paris, a Trojan, had to kidnap her.

Thus began the Trojan War.

. . .

So Celia got out of the car, all right, but she never went to get the apple. As Felix approached her, she tore off her corsage and she kicked off her high-heeled golden dancing shoes, bought, no doubt, like her white dress and maybe her underwear, at prodigious financial sacrifice. And fear and anger and stocking feet, and that magnificent face, made her as astonishing as anyone I have ever encountered in a legend from any culture.

Midland City had a goddess of discord all its own.

This was a goddess who could not dance, would not dance, and hated everybody at the high school. She would like to claw away her face, she told us, so that people would stop seeing things in it that had nothing to do with what she was like inside. She was ready to die at any time, she said, because what men and boys thought about her and tried to do to her made her so ashamed. One of the first things she was going to do when she got to heaven, she said, was to ask somebody what was written on her face and why had it been put there.

. . .

I reconstruct all the things that Celia said that night as Felix and I sit side by side here in Haiti, next to our swimming pool.

She said, we both remember, that black people were kinder and knew more about life than white people did.

She hated the rich. She said that rich people ought to be shot for living the way we did, with a war going on.

And then, leaving her shoes and corsage behind her, she struck out on foot for home.

• • •

She only had about fourteen blocks to go. Felix went after her in the Keedsler, creeping along beside her, begging her to get in. But she ditched him by cutting through a block where the Keedsler couldn't go. And he never found out what happened to her after that. They didn't meet again until 1970, twenty-seven years later. She was then married to Dwayne Hoover, the Pontiac dealer, and Felix had just been fired as president of the National Broadcasting Company.

He had come home to find his roots.

9

My DOUBLE MURDER went like this:

In the spring of 1944, Felix was ordered to active duty in the United States Army. He had just finished up his second semester in the liberal arts at Ohio State. Because of his voice, he had become a very important man on the student radio station, and was also elected vice-president of the freshman class.

He was sworn in at Columbus, but was allowed to spend one more night at home, and part of the next morning, which was Mother's Day, the second Sunday in May.

There were no tears, nor should there have been any, since the Army was going to use him as a radio announcer. But we could have not known that, so we did not cry because Father said that our ancestors had always been proud and happy to serve their country in time of war.

Marco Maritimo, I remember, who by then, in partnership with his brother Gino, had become the biggest building contractor in town, had a son who was drafted at the very same time. And Marco and his wife brought their son over to our house on the night before Mother's Day, and the whole family cried like babies. They didn't care who saw them do it.

They were right to cry, too, as things turned out. Their son Julio would be killed in Germany.

. . .

At dawn on Mother's Day, while Mother was still asleep, Father and Felix and I went out to the rifle range of the Midland County Rod and Gun Club, as we had done at least a hundred times before. It was a Sunday-morning ritual, this discharging of firearms. Although I was only twelve, I had fired rifles and pistols and shotguns of every kind. And there were plenty of other fathers and sons, blazing away and blazing away.

Police Chief Francis X. Morissey was there, I remember, with Bucky, his son. Morissey was one of the bunch who had been goose-hunting with Father and John Fortune back in 1916, when old August Gunther disappeared. Only recently have I learned that it was Morissey who killed old Gunther. He accidentally discharged a ten-gauge shotgun about a foot from Gunther's head.

There was no head left.

So Father and the rest, in order to keep Morissey's life from being ruined by an accident that could have happened to anyone, launched Gunther's body for a voyage down Sugar Creek.

. . .

On the morning of Mother's Day, Father and Felix and I didn't have any exotic weapons along. Since Felix was headed for battle, seemingly, we brought only the Springfield .30-06. The Springfield was no longer the standard American infantry weapon. It had been replaced by the Garand, by the M-1. But it was still used by snipers, because of its superb accuracy.

We all shot well that morning, but I shot better than anybody, which was much commented upon. But only after I had shot a pregnant housewife that afternoon would anybody think to award me my unshakable nickname, Deadeye Dick.

• • •

I got one trophy out on the range that morning, though. When we were through firing, Father said to Felix, "Give your brother Rudy the key."

Felix was puzzled. "What key is that?" he said.

And Father named the Holy of Holies, as far as I was concerned. Felix himself hadn't come into possession of it until he was fifteen years old, and I had never even touched it. "Give him," said Father, "the key to the gun-room door."

• • •

I was certainly very young to receive the key to the gun room. At fifteen, Felix had probably been too young, and I was only twelve. And after I shot the pregnant house-wife, it turned out that Father had only the vaguest idea how old I was. When the police came, I heard him say that I was sixteen or so.

There was this: I was tall for my age. I was tall for any age, since the general population is well under six feet tall, and I was six feet tall. I suppose my pituitary gland was out of kilter for a little while, and then it straightened itself out. I did not become a freakish adult, except for my record as a double murderer, as other people my age more or less caught up with me.

But I was abnormally tall and weak for a time there. I may have been trying to evolve into a superman, and then gave it up in the face of community disapproval.

• • •

So after we got home from the Rod and Gun Club, and I could feel the key to the gun room burning a hole in my pocket, there was yet another proof that I had to be a man now, because Felix was leaving. I had to chop the heads off two chickens for supper that night. This was another privilege which had been accorded Felix, who used to make me watch him.

The place of execution was the stump of the walnut tree, under which Father and old August Gunther had been lunching when the Maritimo brothers arrived in Midland City so long ago. There was a marble bust on a pedestal, which also had to watch. It was another piece of loot from the von Furstenberg estate in Austria. It was a bust of Voltaire.

And Felix used to play God to the chickens, saying in

that voice of his, "If you have any last words to say, now is the time to say them," or "Take your last look at the world," and so on. We didn't raise chickens. A farmer brought in two chickens every Sunday morning, and they had their peepholes closed by a machete in Felix's right hand almost immediately.

Now, with Felix watching, and about to catch a train for Columbus and then a bus for Fort Benning, Georgia, it was up to me to do.

So I grabbed a chicken by its legs, and I flopped it down on the stump, and I said in a voice like a penny whistle, "Take your last look at the world."

Off came its head.

· · ·

Felix kissed Mother, and he shook Father's hand, and he boarded the train at the train station. And then Mother and Father and I had to hurry on home, because we were expecting a very important guest for lunch. She was none other than Eleanor Roosevelt, the wife of the President of the United States. She was visiting war plants in the boondocks to raise morale.

Whenever a famous visitor came to Midland City, he or she was usually brought to Father's studio at one point or another, since there was so little else to see. Usually, they were in Midland City to lecture or sing or play some instrument, or whatever, at the YMCA. That was how I got to meet Nicholas Murray Butler, the president of Columbia University, when I was a boy—and Alexander

Woollcott, the wit and writer and broadcaster, and Cornelia Otis Skinner, the monologist, and Gregor Piatigorsky, the cellist, and on and on.

They all said what Mrs. Roosevelt was about to say: "It's hard to believe I'm in Midland City, Ohio."

Father used to sprinkle a few drops of turpentine and linseed oil on the hot-air registers, so the place would smell like an active studio. When a guest walked in, there was always some classical record on the phonograph, but never German music after Father decided that being a Nazi wasn't such a good idea after all. There was always imported wine, even during the war. There was always Liederkranz cheese, and Father would tell the story of its invention.

And the food was excellent, even when war came and there was strict rationing of meat, since Mary Hoobler was so resourceful with catfish and crayfish from Sugar Creek, and with unrationed parts of animals which other people didn't consider edible.

• • •

Mary Hoobler's chitlins: Take the small intestine of a pig, cut it up into two-inch sections, and wash and wash them, changing the water often, until no fatty particles remain.

Boil them for three or four hours with onions, herbs, and garlic. Serve with greens and grits.

• • •

That is what we served Eleanor Roosevelt for lunch on Mother's Day in 1944—Mary Hoobler's chitlins. She was most appreciative, and she was very democratic, too. She went out into the kitchen and talked to Mary and the other servants there. She had Secret Service agents along, of course, and one of them said to Father, I remember, "I hear you have quite a collection of guns."

So the Secret Service had checked us out. They surely knew, too, that Father had been an admirer of Hitler, but was now reformed, supposedly.

The same man asked what music was playing on the phonograph.

"Chopin," said Father. And then, when the agent appeared to have another question, Father guessed it and answered it: "A Pole," he said. "A Pole, a Pole, a Pole."

And Felix and I, comparing notes here in Haiti, now realize that all our distinguished visitors from out of town had been tipped off that Father was a phony as a painter. Not one of them ever asked to see examples of Father's work.

· · ·

If somebody had been ignorant enough or rude enough to ask, he would have shown them, I suppose, a small canvas clamped into the rugged framework of his easel. His easel was capable of holding a canvas eight feet high and twelve feet wide, I would guess. As I have already said, and particularly in view of the room's other decorations, it was easily mistaken for a guillotine.

The small canvas, whose back was turned toward visitors, was where a guillotine's fallen blade might be. It was the only picture I ever saw on the easel, as long as Father and I were on the same planet together, and some of our guests must have gone to the trouble of looking at its face. I think Mrs. Roosevelt did. I am sure the Secret Service agents did. They wanted to see everything.

And what they saw on that canvas were brushstrokes laid down exuberantly and confidently, and promisingly, too, in prewar Vienna, when Father was only twenty years old. It was only a sketch so far—of a nude model in the studio he rented after he moved out of the home of our relatives over there. There was a skylight. There was wine and cheese and bread on a checkered tablecloth.

Was Mother jealous of that naked model? No. How could she be? When that picture was begun, Mother was only eleven years old.

• • •

That rough sketch was the only respectable piece of artwork by my father that I ever saw. After he died in 1960, and Mother and I moved into our little two bedroom shitbox out in Avondale, we hung it over our fireplace. That was the same fireplace that would eventually kill Mother, since its mantelpiece had been made with radioactive cement left over from the Manhattan Project, from the atomic bomb project in World War Two.

It is still somewhere in the shitbox, I presume, since Midland City is now being protected against looters by the

National Guard. And its special meaning for me is this: It is proof that sometime back when my father was a young, young man, he must have had a moment or two when he felt that he might have reason to take himself and his life seriously.

I can hear him saying to himself in astonishment, after he had roughed in that promising painting: "My God! I'm a painter after all!"

Which he wasn't.

. . .

So, during a lunch of chitlins, topped off with coffee and crackers and Liederkranz, Mrs. Roosevelt told us how proud and unselfish and energetic the men and women were over the tank-assembly line at Green Diamond Plow. They were working night and day over there. And even at lunchtime of Mother's Day, the studio trembled as tanks rumbled by outside. The tanks were on the way to the proving ground which used to be John Fortune's dairy farm, and which would later become the Maritimo Brother's jumble of little shitboxes known as Avondale.

Mrs. Roosevelt knew that Felix had just left for the Army, and she prayed that he would be safe. She said that the hardest part of her husband's job was that there was no way to win a battle without many persons being injured or killed.

Like Father, she assumed, because I was so tall, that I must be about sixteen. Anyway, she guessed it was touch-

and-go whether I myself would be drafted by and by. She certainly hoped not.

For my own part, I hoped that my voice changed before then.

She said that there would be a wonderful new world when the war was won. Everybody who needed food or medicine would get it, and people could say anything they wanted, and could choose any religion that appealed to them. Leaders wouldn't dare to be unjust anymore, since all the other countries would gang up on them. For this reason, there could never be another Hitler. He would be squashed like a bug before he got very far.

And then Father asked me if I had cleaned the Springfield rifle yet. That was something I got along with the key to the gun room: the duty to clean the guns.

Felix says now that Father made such an honor and fetish out of the key to the gun room because he was too lazy to ever clean a gun.

• • •

Mrs. Roosevelt, I remember, made some polite inquiry about my familiarity with firearms. And it was news to Mother, too, that I had the key to the gun room now.

So Father told them both that Felix and I knew more about small arms than most professional soldiers, and he said most of the things the National Rifle Association still says about how natural and beautiful it is for Americans to have love affairs with guns. He said that he had taught Felix and me about guns when we were so young in order to make our safety habits second nature. "My boys will never have a shooting accident," he said, "because their respect for weapons has become a part of their nervous systems."

I wasn't about to say so, but I had some doubts at that point about the gun safety habits of Felix, and of his friend Bucky Morissey, too—the son of the chief of police. For the past couple of years, anyway, Felix and Bucky, without Father's knowledge, had been helping themselves to various weapons in the gun room, and had picked off crows perched on headstones in Calvary Cemetery, and had cut off telephone service to several farms by shooting insulators along the Sheperdstown Turnpike, and had blasted God-only-knows how many mailboxes all over the county, and had actually loosed a couple of rounds at a herd of sheep out near Sacred Miracle Cave.

Also: After a big Thanksgiving Day football game between Midland City and Sheperdstown, a bunch of Shepherdstown tough guys had caught Felix and Bucky walking home from the football field. They were going to beat up Felix and Bucky, but Felix dispersed them by pulling from the belt under his jacket a fully loaded Colt .45 automatic.

He wasn't kidding around.

• • •

But Father knew nothing of this, obviously, as he blathered on about safety habits. And, after Mrs. Roosevelt made her departure, he sent me up to the gun room, to clean the Springfield without further delay.

So this was Mother's Day to most people, but to me it was the day during which, ready or not, I had been initiated into manhood. I had killed the chickens. Now I had been made master of all these guns and all this ammunition. It was something to savor. It was something to think about and I had the Springfield in my arms. It loved to be held. It was born to be held.

I liked it so much, and it liked me so much, since I had fired it so well that morning, that I took it with me when I climbed the ladder up into the cupola. I wanted to sit up there for a while, and look out over the roofs of the town, supposing that my brother might be going to his death, and hearing and feeling the tanks in the street below. Ah, sweet mystery of life.

I had a clip of ammunition in my breast pocket. It had been there since morning. It felt good. So I pushed it down into the rifle's magazine, since I knew the rifle enjoyed that so. It just ate up those cartridges.

I slid forward the bolt, which caught the topmost cartridge and delivered it into the chamber. I locked the bolt. Now the rifle was cocked, with a live cartridge snugly home.

For a person as familiar with firearms as I was, this represented no commitment whatsoever. I could let down the hammer gently, without firing the cartridge. And then I could withdraw the bolt, which would extract the live cartridge and throw it away.

But I squeezed the trigger instead.

10

ELEANOR ROOSEVELT, with her dreams of a better world than this one, was well on her way to some other small city by then—to raise morale. So she never got to hear me shoot.

Mother and Father heard me shoot. So did some of the neighbors. But nobody could be sure of what he or she had heard, with the tanks making such an uproar on their way to the proving ground. Their new engines backfired plenty the first time they tasted petroleum.

Father came upstairs to find out if I was all right. I was better than that. I was at one with the universe. I heard him coming, but I was unconcerned—even though I was still at an open window in the cupola with the Springfield in my arms.

He asked me if I had heard a bang. I said I had.

He asked me if I knew what the bang had been. I said, "No."

I took my own sweet time about descending from the

cupola. Firing the Springfield over the city was now part of my treasure-house of memories.

I hadn't aimed at anything. If I thought of the bullet's hitting anything, I don't remember now. I was the great marksman, anyway. If I aimed at nothing, then nothing is what I would hit.

The bullet was a symbol, and nobody was ever hurt by a symbol. It was a farewell to my childhood and a confirmation of my manhood.

Why didn't I use a blank cartridge? What kind of a symbol would that have been?

• • •

I put the spent cartridge in a wastebasket for spent cartridges, which would be given to a scrap drive. It became a member of that great wartime fraternity, Cartridge Cases Anonymous.

I took the Springfield apart and cleaned it. I put it back together again, which I could have done when blindfolded, and I restored it to its rack.

What a friend it had been to me.

I rejoined polite society downstairs, locking the gun room behind me. All those guns weren't for just anybody to handle. Some people were fools where guns were concerned.

• • •

So I helped Mary Hoobler clean up after Mrs. Roosevelt. My participation in housework had become invisible. My parents had always had servants, after all, sort of ghostly people. Mother and Father were incurious as to who it was, exactly, who brought something or took something away.

I certainly wasn't effeminate. I had no interest in dressing like a girl, and I was a good shot, and I played a little football and baseball and so on. What if I liked cooking? The greatest cooks in the world were men.

Out in the kitchen, where Mary Hoobler washed and I dried, Mary said that the most important thing in her life had now happened. She had met Mrs. Roosevelt, and she would tell her grandchildren about it, and everything for her was downhill now. Nothing that important could ever happen to her again.

The front doorbell rang. The great carriage-house doors had of course been closed and bolted after the fiasco with poor Celia Hildreth the year before. We had an ordinary front door again.

So I answered the door. Mother and Father never answered the door. It was police chief Morissey out there. He looked very unhappy and secretive. He told me that he didn't want to come in, and he particularly didn't want to disturb my mother—so I was to tell Father to come out for a talk with him. He said I should be in on it, too.

I give my word of honor: I had not the slightest inkling of what the trouble might be.

So I got Father. He and Chief Morissey and I were going to do some more man business, business that women might be better off not hearing about. They might not understand. I was drying my hands on a tea towel.

And Morissey himself, as I know now but didn't know then, had accidentally killed August Gunther with a firearm when he was young.

And he said quietly to Father and me that Eloise Metzger, the pregnant wife of the city editor of the *Bugle-Observer*, George Metzger, had just been shot dead while running a vacuum cleaner in the guest room on the second floor of her home over on Harrison Avenue, about eight blocks away. There was a bullet hole in the window.

Her family downstairs had become worried when the vacuum cleaner went on running and running without being dragged around at all.

Chief Morissey said that Mrs. Metzger couldn't have felt any pain, since the bullet got her right between the eyes. She never knew what hit her.

The bullet had been recovered from the guest-room floor, and it was virtually undamaged, thanks to its copper jacket, in spite of all it had been through.

"Now I am asking you two as an old friend of the family," said Morissey, "and before any official investigation has begun, and I am just another human being and family man standing here before you: Does either one of you have any idea where a .30-caliber copper-jacketed rifle bullet could have come from about an hour ago?"

I died.

But I didn't die.

. . .

Father knew exactly where it had come from. He had heard the bang. He had seen me at the top of the ladder in the cupola, with the Springfield in my arms.

He made a wet hiss, sucking in air through his clenched teeth. It is the sound stoics make when they have been hurt a good deal. He said, "Oh, Jesus."

"Yes," said Morissey. And everything about his manner said that no possible good could come from our being made to suffer for this unfortunate accident, which could have happened to anyone. He, for one, would do all in his power to make whatever we had done somehow understandable and acceptable to the community. Perhaps, even, we could convince the community that the bullet had come from somewhere else.

We certainly didn't have the only .30-caliber rifle in town.

I myself began to feel a little better. Here was this wise and powerful adult, the chief of police, no less, and he clearly believed that I had done no bad thing. I was unlucky. I would never be that unlucky again. That was for sure.

I took a deep breath. That was for sure.

11

So EVERYTHING was going to be okay.

And Father's life and Mother's life and my life would have been okay, I firmly believe, if it weren't for what Father did next.

He felt that, given who he was, he had no option other than to behave nobly. "The boy did it," he said, "but it is I who am to blame."

"Now, just a minute, Otto—" Morissey cautioned him.

But Father was off and running, into the house, shouting to Mother and Mary Hoobler and anybody else who could hear him, "I am to blame! I am to blame!"

And more police came, not meaning to arrest me or Father, or to even question us, but simply to report to Morissey. They certainly weren't going to do anything mean, unless Morissey told them to.

So they heard Father's confession, too: "I am to blame!"

. . .

What, incidentally, was a pregnant mother of two doing, operating a vacuum cleaner on Mother's Day? She was practically asking for a bullet between the eyes, wasn't she?

. . .

Felix missed all the fun, of course, since he was on a troop bus bound for Georgia. He had been put in charge of his particular bus, because of his commanding vocal cords—but that was pretty small stuff compared to what Father and I were doing.

And Felix has made surprisingly few comments over the years on that fateful Mother's Day. Just now, though, here in Haiti, he said to me, "You know why the old man confessed?"

"No," I said.

"It was the first truly consequential adventure life had ever offered him. He was going to make the most of it. At last something was happening to him! He would keep it going as long as he could!"

. . .

Father really did make quite a show of it. Not only did he make an unnecessary confession, but then he took a hammer and a prybar and a chisel, and the machete I had used on the chickens, and he went clumping upstairs to the gun-room door. He himself had a key, but he didn't use it. He hacked and smashed the lock away.

Everybody was too awed to stop him.

And never, may I say, would the moment come when he would give the tiniest crumb of guilt to me. The guilt was all his, and would remain entirely, exclusively his for the rest of his life. So I was just another bleak and innocent onlooker, along with Mother and Mary Hoobler and Chief Morissey, and maybe eight small-city cops.

He broke all his guns, just whaled away at them in their racks with the hammer. He at least bent or dented all of them. A few old-timers shattered. What would those guns be worth today, if Felix and I had inherited them? I will guess a hundred thousand dollars or more.

Father ascended the ladder into the cupola, where I had been so recently. He there accomplished what Marco Maritimo later said should have been impossible for one man with such small and inappropriate tools. He cut away the base of the cupola, and he capsized it. It twisted free from its last few feeble moorings, and it went bounding down the slate roof, and it went crashing, weather vane and all, onto Chief Morrisey's police car in the driveway below.

There was silence after that.

I and the rest of Father's audience were at the foot of the gun-room ladder, looking up. What a hair-raising melodrama Father had given to Midland City, Ohio. And it was over now. There the leading character was above us, crimson faced and panting, but somehow most satisfied, too, exposed to wind and sky.

12

I THINK FATHER was surprised when he and I were taken away to jail after that. He never said anything to confirm this, but I think, and Felix agrees, that he was sufficiently adrift to imagine that wrecking the guns and decapitating the house would somehow settle everything. He intended to pay for his crime, the trusting of a child with firearms and live ammunition, before the bill could even be presented. What class!

That was surely one of the messages his pose at the top of the ladder, against the sky, had conveyed to me, and I had been glad to believe it: "Paid in full, by God—paid in full!"

But they took us down to the hoosegow.

Mother went to bed, and didn't get out of it for a week.

Marco and Gino Maritimo, who had dozens of workmen at their command, came over to put a tar-paper cap on the big hole in the roof personally, before the sun went down. Nobody had called them. Everybody in town had heard about the kinds of trouble we were in by then. Most of the sympathy, naturally enough, was going to the husband and two children of the woman I had shot.

And Eloise Metzger had been pregnant—which, as I have already said, made me a double murderer.

You know what it says in the Bible? "Thou shalt not kill."

. . .

Chief Morissey gave up on rescuing Father and me, since Father seemed to find it so rewarding to damn and doom himself. Throwing up his hands and departing, he left us in the hands of a mild old lieutenant and a stenographer. Father told me to describe exactly how I had fired the rifle, and I answered simply and truthfully. The stenographer wrote it down.

And then Father had this to say, for his own part, which was also duly recorded: "This is only a boy here. His mother and I are morally and legally responsible for his actions, except when it comes to the handling of firearms. I alone am responsible for whatever he does with guns, and I alone am responsible for the terrible accident which happened this afternoon. He has been a good boy up to now, and will be a sturdy and decent man in due time. I have no words of reproach to utter to him now. I gave him a gun and ammunition when he was much too young to have them without any supervision." He had by then found out I was only twelve, and not sixteen or so. "Leave him out of this. Leave my poor wife out of this. I, Otto Waltz, being of sound mind, do now declare under oath and in fear for my soul, that I alone am to blame."

• • •

And I think he was surprised, again, when we weren't allowed to go home after that. What more could anybody want after a confession that orotund?

But he was led off to cells in the basement of police headquarters, and I was taken to a much smaller cell-block on the top floor, the third floor, which was reserved for women and for children under the age of sixteen. There was only one other prisoner up there, a black woman from out of town, who had been taken off a Greyhound bus after beating up the white driver. She was from the Deep South, and she was the one who introduced me to the idea of birth's being an opening peephole, and of death's being when that peephole closes again.

The idea must have been ordinary, back wherever it was she came from. She said she was sorry she had beat up the bus driver, who had spoken to her insultingly because of her race. "I didn't ask my peephole to open. It just open one day, and I hear the people saying, 'That's a black one there. Unlucky to be black.' And that poor driver they took off to the hospital, his peephole done open, and he hear the people saying, 'That's a white one there. Lucky to be white.' "

A while later she sad, "My peephole open, I see this woman, I say, 'Who you?' She say, 'I's you mama.' I say, 'How we doing, Mama?' She say, 'Ain't doing good. Ain't got no money, ain't got no work, ain't got no house, your daddy on the chain gang, and I already got seven other children whose peepholes opened up on them.' And I said, 'Mama, if you know how to close up my peephole again, you just go ahead and do it.' And she say, 'Don't you tempt me like that, child. That's the devil talking through you.' "

She asked me what a white boy in nice clothes was doing in jail. So I told her that I had had an accident while cleaning a rifle. It had gone off somehow, and killed a woman far away. I was beginning to work up a defense, even if Father didn't believe in making one.

"Oh, my Lord," she said, "—you done closed a peephole. That can't feel good. That can't feel good."

• • •

It felt to me then as though my peephole had just opened, and I wasn't even used to all the sights and sounds yet, but my father had already chopped the top off our house, and everybody was saying I was a killer. This was a planet where everything happened much too fast.

I could hardly catch my breath.

But police headquarters seemed quiet enough. Not much could happen on a Sunday night.

How common was it to have a known killer in a cell in Midland City? I had no way of knowing then, but I have since looked up the crime statistics for 1944. A killer was quite a novelty. There were only eight detected homicides of any sort. Three were drunken driving accidents. One was a sober driving accident. One was a fight in a black nightclub. One was a fight in a white bar. One was the shooting of a brother-in-law mistaken for a burglar. And there was Eloise Metzger and me.

Because of my age, I could not be prosecuted. Only Father could be prosecuted. Chief Morissey had explained that to me very early in the game—at a time when he thought there was all sorts of hope for both Father and me. So I felt safe, although embarrassed.

Little did I know that Morissey had meanwhile concluded that Father and I were dangerous imbeciles, since we seemed determined to confess to far more than was necessary, to inflame the community by seeming almost proud of my having shot Mrs. Metzger. Mrs. Metzger and her survivors were nothing. Father and I, on the other hand, confessing so boisterously, appeared to think we were movies stars.

We were no longer protected by Morissey, and a tentative, moody, slow-motion and incomplete lynching was about to begin. First, as I lay facedown on my cot, trying to blot out what my life had come to be, a bucket of ice-cold water was thrown all over me.

Two policemen hoisted me to my feet and shackled my hands behind my back. They put leg-irons on my ankles, and they dragged me into an office on the same floor, in order to fingerprint me, they said.

I was tall, but I was weak, and I weighed about as much as a box of kitchen matches. The one manly feat of strength of which I was capable was the mastery of a bucking gun. Instructed by my father and my brother on the range at the Rod and Gun Club, I had learned to knit together whatever strength and weight I had so as to absorb any shock a man-sized rifle or shotgun or pistol might wish to deal to me—to absorb it with amusement and satisfaction, and to get ready to fire again and again.

I was not only fingerprinted. I was faceprinted, too. The police pushed my hand and then my face into a shallow pan of gummy black ink.

I was straightened up, and one of the policemen commented that I was a proper-looking nigger now. Until that moment, I had been willing to believe that policemen were my best friends and everybody's best friends.

• • •

I was about to be put on display to concerned members of the community—in a holding pen for suspected criminals awaiting trial, in the basement of the old County Courthouse across the street. It was ten at night. It was still Mother's Day. The courthouse was empty. The upper floors would remain dark. Only the basement lights would be on.

It was the feeling of the police that I should not look good, and that I bear some marks of their displeasure with what I had done. But they couldn't beat me up, as they might have beaten up an adult offender, since that might evoke sympathy. So they had rolled my face in goo.

All this was in clear violation of the Bill of Rights of the Constitution of the United States.

· · ·

So I was put in this large cage in the basement of the courthouse. It was rectangular, and made of heavy-duty mesh fencing and vertical iron pipes. It was open to observers on all four sides. It contained wooden benches for about thirty people, I would say. There were plenty of cuspidors, but no toilet. Any caged person having to go to the toilet had to say so, and then to be escorted to a nearby lavatory.

I was unshackled.

The audience had yet to arrive, but the policemen who had brought me there, and who were now separated from me by wire, showed me what I was going to see a lot of—fingers hooked through the mesh. Person after person, bellying up to the wire for a good look at me, would, almost automatically, hook his or her fingers through the mesh.

Look at the monkey.

· · ·

Who were the people who came to look at the monkey? Many were simply friends or relatives of policemen, responding to oral invitations along these lines, no doubt: "If you want to see the kid who shot that pregnant woman this afternoon, we've got him in the courthouse basement. I can get you in. Keep it under your hat, though. Don't tell anyone else. We don't want a mob to form."

But the honored visitors were substantial citizens, grave community leaders with a presumed need to know everything. There was something the policeman on the telephone thought it important for them to see—so they had better see it. Duty called. Some brought members of their families. I even remember a babe in arms.

So far as I know, only two people told the inviters that displaying a boy in a cage was a terrible thing to do, and stunk of the Middle Ages and so on. They were, of course, Gino and Marco Maritimo, virtually our family's only steadfast friends. And I know of this only because the brothers themselves told me about it. They had received the obscene invitation, offered as though nothing could be more civilized, soon after capping the hole in our roof where the cupola had been.

. . .

I have mentioned Alexander Woollcott, the writer and wit and broadcaster and so on, who was a guest at our house one time. He coined that wonderful epithet for writers, "ink-stained wretches."

He should have seen me in my cage.

. . .

I sat on the same bench for two hours. I said nothing, no matter what was said to me. Sometimes I sat bolt upright. Sometimes I bent over, with my head down and my inky hands over my inky ears or eyes. Toward the end, my bladder was full to bursting. I peed in my pants rather than speak. Why not? I was a geek. I was a wild man from Borneo.

. . .

I have since determined, from talking to old, old people, that I was the only Midland City criminal to have been put on public display since the days of public hangings on the courthouse lawn. My punishment was more than cruel and unusual. It was unique. But it made sense to just about everybody—with the exception of the Maritimo brothers, as I have said, and, surprisingly, George Metzger, the city editor of the *Bugle-Observer,* the husband of the woman I had killed that afternoon.

Before George Metzger arrived, though, members of my audience behaved as though they were quite accustomed to taunting bad people. They may have done a lot of it in their dreams. They clearly felt entitled to respectful attention from me.

So I heard a lot of things like "Hey you—it's you I'm talking to. Yes you!" and "God damn it, you look me in the eye, you son of a bitch," and so on.

I was told about friends or relatives who had been hurt or killed in the war. Some of the casualties were victims of industrial accidents right there at home. The moral arithmetic was simple. Here all those soldiers and sailors and workers in war plants were risking their all to add more goodness to the world, whereas I had just subtracted some.

What was my own opinion of myself? I thought I was a defective human being, and that I shouldn't even be on

this planet anymore. Anybody who would fire a Springfield .30-06 over the rooftops of a city had to have a screw
loose.

If I had begun to reply to the people, I think that's
what I would have babbled over and over again: "I have a
screw loose somewhere, I have a screw loose somewhere, I
have a screw loose somewhere."

. . .

Celia Hildreth came by the cage. I hadn't seen her for
a year, since the awful night of the senior prom, but I had
no trouble recognizing her. She was still the most beautiful
woman in town. I can't imagine that the police had seen fit
to invite her. It was her escort, surely, who had been invited. She was on the arm of Dwayne Hoover, who was
then some sort of civilian inspector for the Army Air
Corps, I think.

Something had kept him out of uniform. I knew who
he was because he was good with automobiles, and Father
had hired him from time to time to do some work on the
Keedsler. Dwayne would eventually marry Celia and become the most successful automobile dealer in the area.

Celia would commit suicide by eating Drāno, a
drain-clearing compound of lye and zinc chips, in 1970,
twelve years ago now. She killed herself in the most horrible way I can think of—a few months before the dedication of the Mildred Barry Memorial Center for the Arts.

Celia knew the arts center was going to open, and the
newspaper and the radio station and the politicians and so

on all said what a difference it was going to make in the quality of life in Midland City. But there was the can of Drāno, with all its dire warnings, and she just couldn't wait around anymore.

I have seen unhappiness in my time.

13

Now that I have known Haiti, with its voodoo-ism, with its curses and charms and zombies and good and bad spirits which can inhabit anybody or anything, and so on, I wonder if it mattered much that it was I who was in the cage in the basement of the old courthouse so long ago. A curiously carved bone or stick, or a dried mud doll with straw hair would have served as well as I did, there on the bench, as long as the community believed, as Midland City believed of me, that it was a package of evil magic.

Everybody could feel safe for a while. Bad luck was caged. There was bad luck, cringing on the bench in there.

See for yourself.

• • •

At midnight, all the civilians were shooed out of the basement. "That's it, folks," said the police, and "Show's over, folks," and so on. They were frank to call me a show. I was regional theater.

But I wasn't let out of the cage. It would have been

nice to take a bath, and to go to bed between clean sheets, and to sleep until I died.

There was more to come. Six policemen were still in the basement with me—three in uniform and three in plain clothes, and all with pistols. I could name the manufacturers of the pistols, and their calibers. There wasn't a pistol there that I couldn't have taken apart and cleaned properly, and put together again. I knew where the drops of oil should go. If they had put their pistols in my hands, I could have made them this guarantee: The pistols would never jam.

It can be a very frustrating thing if a pistol jams.

The six remaining policemen were the producers of the Rudy Waltz Snow, and their poses in the basement indicated that we had reached an intermission, that there was more to come. They ignored me for the moment, as though a curtain had descended.

They were electrified by a call from upstairs. "He's here!" was the call, as a door upstairs opened and shut. They echoed that. "He's here, he's here." They wouldn't say who it was, but it was somebody somehow marvelous. Now I heard his footsteps on the stairs.

I thought it might be an executioner. I thought it might be Police Chief Francis X. Morissey, that old family friend, who had yet to show himself. I thought it might be my father.

It was George Metzger, the thirty-five-year-old widower of the woman I had shot. He was fifteen years younger than I am now, a mere spring chicken—but, as children will, I saw him as an old man. He was bald on top. He was skinny, and his posture was bad, and he was dressed like almost no other man in Midland City—in gray flannel trousers and a tweed sport coat, what I would recognize much later at Ohio State as the uniform of an English professor. All he did was write and edit at the *Bugle-Observer* all day long.

I did not know who he was. He had never been to our house. He had been in town only a year. He was a newspaper gypsy. He had been hired away from the *Indianapolis Times*. It would come out at legal proceedings later on that he was born to poor parents in Kenosha, Wisconsin, and had put himself through Harvard, and that he had twice worked his way to Europe on cattle boats. The adverse information about him, which was brought out by our lawyer, was that he had once belonged to the Communist party, and had attempted to enlist in the Abraham Lincoln Brigade during the Spanish Civil War.

He wore horn-rimmed spectacles, and his eyes were red from crying, or maybe from too much cigarette smoke. He was smoking when he came down the stairs, followed by the detective who had gone to get him. He behaved as though he himself were a criminal, puffing on the same cigarette he would be smoking when he was propped against the basement wall in front of a firing squad.

I wouldn't have been surprised if the police had shot this unhappy stranger while I watched. I was beyond surprise. I am still beyond surprise. The consequences of my having shot a pregnant woman were bound to be complicated beyond belief.

How can I bear to remember that first confrontation with George Metzger? I have this trick for dealing with all my worst memories. I insist that they are plays. The characters are actors. Their speeches and movements are stylized, arch. I am in the presence of art.

So:

The curtain rises on a basement at midnight. Six POLICEMEN *stand around the walls.* RUDY, *a boy, covered with ink, is in a cage in the middle of the room. Down the stairs, smoking a cigarette, comes* GEORGE METZGER, *whose wife has just been shot by the boy. He is followed by a* DETECTIVE, *who has the air of a master of ceremonies. The* POLICE *are fascinated by what is about to happen. It is bound to be interesting.*

METZGER *(appalled by* RUDY's *appearance):* Oh, my God. What is it?

DETECTIVE: That's what shot your wife, Mr. Metzger.

METZGER: What have you done to him?

DETECTIVE: Don't worry about him. He's fine. You want him to sing and dance? We can make him sing and dance.

METZGER: I'm sure. *(Pause)* All right. I've looked at him. Will you take me back home to my children now?

DETECTIVE: We were hoping you'd have a few words to say to him.

METZGER: Is that required?

DETECTIVE: No, sir. But the boys and me here—we figured you should have this golden opportunity.

METZGER: It sounded so official—that I was to come with
you. *(Catching on, troubled)* This is not an official as-
sembly. This is—*(Pause)* informal.

DETECTIVE: Nobody's even here. I'm home in bed, you're
home in bed. All the other boys are home in bed.
Ain't that right, boys?

(POLICEMEN *assent variously, making snoring sounds and so on.*)

METZGER *(morbidly curious):* What would it please you gen-
tlemen to have me do?

DETECTIVE: If you was to grab a gun away from one of us,
and it was to go off, and if the bullet was to hit young
Mr. Rich Nazi Shitface there, I wouldn't blame you.
But it would be hard for us to clean up the mess afterwards. A mess like that can go on and on.

METZGER: So I should limit my assault to words, you think?

DETECTIVE: Some people talk with their hands and feet.

METZGER: I should beat him up.

DETECTIVE: Heavens to Betsy, no. How could you think
such a thing?

(POLICEMEN *display mock horror at the thought of a beating.*)

METZGER: Just asking.

DETECTIVE: Get him out here, boys.

(Two POLICEMEN *hasten to unlock the cage and drag* RUDY *out of it.* RUDY *struggles in terror.)*

RUDY: It was an accident! I'm sorry! I didn't know! *(and so on)*

(The two POLICEMEN *hold* RUDY *in front of* METZGER, *so that* METZGER *can hit and kick him as much as he likes.)*

DETECTIVE *(to both* RUDY *and* METZGER): A lot of people fall down stairs. We have to take them to the hospital afterwards. It's a very common accident. Up to now, it's happened with mean drunks and to niggers who don't seem to understand their place. We never had a smart-ass kid murderer on our hands before.

METZGER *(uninterested in doing anything, giving up on life):* What a day this has been.

DETECTIVE: Don't want to hit him where it shows? Pull his pants down, boys, so this man can whap his ass. *(PO-LICEMEN pull down* RUDY's *pants, turn him around, and bend him over)* Somebody get this man something to whap an ass with.

(Unoccupied POLICEMEN *search for a suitable whip.* POLICEMAN ONE *finds a piece of cable on the floor about two feet long, proudly brings it to* METZGER, *who accepts it listlessly.)*

METZGER: Many thanks.
POLICEMAN ONE: Any time.
RUDY: I'm sorry! It was an accident!

(All wait in silence for the first blow. METZGER *does not move, but speaks to a higher power instead.)*

METZGER: God—there should not be animals like us. There should be no lives like ours.

*(*METZGER *drops the whip, turns, walks to the stairs, clumps up them. Nobody moves. A door upstairs opens and closes.* RUDY *is still bent over. Twenty seconds pass.)*

POLICEMAN ONE *(in a dream):* Jesus—how's he gonna get home?
DETECTIVE *(in a dream):* Walk. It's nice out.
POLICEMAN ONE: How far away does he live?
DETECTIVE: Six blocks from here.

(Curtain.)

• • •

It wasn't exactly like that, of course. I don't have total recall. It was a lot like that.

I was allowed to straighten up and pull up my pants. I had such a little pecker then. They still wouldn't let me wash, but Mr. Metzger had succeeded in warning these fundamentally innocent, hayseed policemen of how crazy they had become.

So I wasn't bopped around much anymore, and pretty soon I would be taken home to my mother.

Since it was Mr. Metzger's wife I had shot, he had the power not only to make the police take it easy with me, but to persuade the whole town to more or less forgive me. This he did—in a very short statement which appeared on the front page of the *Bugle-Observer,* bordered in black, a day and a half after my moment of fatal carelessness:

"My wife has been killed by a machine which should never have come into the hands of any human being. It is called a firearm. It makes the blackest of all human wishes come true at once, at a distance: that something die.

"There is evil for you.

"We cannot get rid of mankind's fleetingly wicked wishes. We can get rid of the machines that make them come true.

"I give you a holy word: DISARM."

14

WHILE I WAS in the cage, another bunch of policeman had been beating up Father in the police station across the street. He should never have refused the easy way out which Police Chief Morissey had offered him. But it was too late now.

The police actually threw him down a flight of stairs. They didn't just pretend that was what had happened to him. There was a lot of confused racist talk, evidently. Father would later remember lying at the bottom of the stairs, with somebody standing over him and asking him, "Hey, Nazi—how does it feel to be a nigger now?"

They brought me to see him after my confrontation with George Metzger. He was in a room in the basement, all bunged up, and entirely broken in spirit.

"Look at your rotten father," he said. "What a worthless man I am." If he was curious about my condition, he gave no sign of it. He was so theatrically absorbed by his own helplessness and worthlessness that I don't think he even noticed that his own son was all covered with ink. Nor did he ever ask me what I had just been through.

Nor did he consider the propriety of my hearing what he was determined to confess next, which was how his character had been corrupted at an early age by liquor and whores. I would never have known of the wild times he and old August Gunther used to have, when they were supposedly visiting museums and studios. Felix would never have known of them, if I hadn't told him. Mother never did know, I'm sure. I certainly never told her.

And that might have been bearable information for a twelve-year-old, since it had all happened so long ago. But then Father went on to say that he *still* patronized prostitutes regularly, although he had the most wonderful wife in the world.

He was all in pieces.

. . .

The police had become subdued by then. Some of them may have been wondering what on earth they thought they had been doing.

Word may have come down from Chief Morissey that enough was enough. Father and I had no lawyer to secure our rights for us. Father refused to call a lawyer. But the district attorney or somebody must have said that I should be sent home without any further monkey business.

Anyway—after being shown my father, I was told to sit on a hard bench in a corridor and wait. I was left all alone, still covered with ink. I could have walked out of there. Policemen would come by, and hardly give me a glance.

And then a young one in uniform stopped in front of me, acting like somebody who had been told to carry the garbage out, and he said, "On your feet, killer. I've got orders to take you home."

There was a clock on the wall. It was one o'clock in the morning. The law was through with me, except as a witness. Under the law, I was only a witness to my father's crime of criminal negligence. There would be a coroner's inquest. I would have to testify.

. . .

So this ordinary patrolman drove me home. He kept his eye on the road, but his thoughts were all of me. He said that I would have to think about Mrs. Metzger, lying cold in the ground, for the rest of my life, and that, if he were me, he would probably commit suicide. He said that he expected some relative of Mrs. Metzger would get me sooner or later, when I least expected it—maybe the very next day, or maybe when I was a man, full of hopes and good prospects, and with a family of my own. Whoever did it, he said, would probably want me to suffer some.

I would have been too addled, too close to death, to get his name, if he hadn't insisted that I learn it. It was Anthony Squires, and he said it was important that I commit it to memory, since I would undoubtedly want to make a complaint about him, since policemen were expected to speak politely at all times, and that, before he got me home, he was going to call me a little Nazi cocksucker and a dab of catshit and he hadn't decided what all yet.

He explained, too, why he wasn't in the armed forces, even though he was only twenty-four years old. Both his eardrums were broken, he said, because his father and mother used to beat him up all the time. "They held my hand over the fire of a gas range once," he said. "You ever had that done to you?"

"No," I said.

"High time," he said. "Or too late, maybe. That's locking the barn after the horse is stolen."

And I of course reconstruct this conversation from a leaky old memory. It went something like that. I can give my word of honor that one thing was said, however: "You know what I'm going to call you from now on," he said, "and what I'm going to tell everybody else to call you?"

"No," I said.

And he said, "Deadeye Dick."

• • •

He did not accompany me to the door of our home, which was dark inside. There was no moon. His headlights picked out a strange broken form in the driveway. It hadn't been there on the previous morning. It was of course the wreckage of the cupola and the famous weather vane. It had been pulled off the top of the police chief's car and left there in the driveway.

The front door was locked, which wasn't unusual. It was always locked at night, since the neighborhood had de-

teriorated so, and since we had so many supposed art treasures inside. I had a key in my pocket, but it wasn't the right
key.

It was the key to the gun-room door.

• • •

Patrolman Anthony Squires, incidentally, would many
years later become chief of detectives, and then suffer a nervous breakdown. He is dead now. He was working as a part-
time bartender at the new Holiday Inn when he had his
peephole closed by ye olde neutron bomb.

• • •

Mrs. Gino Maritimo's *spuma di cioccolata:* Break up six
ounces of semisweet chocolate in a saucepan. Melt it in a
250-degree oven.

Add two teaspoons of sugar to four egg yolks, and beat
the mixture until it is pale yellow. Then mix in the melted
chocolate, a quarter cup of strong coffee, and two tablespoons of rum.

Whip two-thirds of a cup of cold, heavy whipping
cream until it is stiff. Fold it into the mixture.

Whip four egg whites until they form stiff peaks, then
fold them into the mixture. Stir the mixture ever so gently,
then spoon it into cups, each cup a serving. Refrigerate for
twelve hours.

Serves six.

• • •

So Mother's Day of 1944 was over. I was locked out of my own home as the wee hours of a new day began. I shuffled through the darkness to our back door, the only other door. That, too, was locked.

No one had been told to expect me, and we had no servants who lived with us. So there was only my mother to awaken inside. I did not want to see her.

I had not cried yet about what I had done, and about all that had been done to me. Now I cried, standing outside the back door.

I grieved so noisily that dogs barked at me.

Someone inside the fortress manipulated the brass jewelry of the back door's lock. The door opened for me. There stood my mother, Emma, who was herself a child. Outside of school, she had never had any responsibilities, any work to do. Her servants had raised her children. She was purely ornamental.

Nothing bad was supposed to happen to her—ever. But here she was in a thin bathrobe now, without her husband or servants, or her basso profundo elder son. And there I was, her gangling, flute-voiced younger son, a murderer.

She wasn't about to hug me, or cover my inky head with kisses. She was not what I would call demonstrative. When Felix went off to war, she shook his hand by way of encouragement—and then blew a kiss to him when his train was a half a mile away.

And, oh, Lord, I don't mean to make a villain of this woman, with whom I spent so many years. After Father died, I would be paired off with her, like a husband with a wife. We had each other, and that was about all we had. She wasn't wicked. She simply wasn't useful.

"What is that all over you?" she said. She meant the ink. She was protecting herself. She didn't want to get it on her, too.

She was so far from imagining what I might want that she did not even get out of the doorway so I could come inside. I wanted to get into my bed and pull the covers over my head. That was my plan. That is still pretty much my plan.

So, keeping me outside, and not even sure whether she wanted to let me in or not, seemingly, she asked me when Father was coming home, and whether everything was going to be all right now, and so on.

She needed good news, so I gave it to her. I said that I was fine, and that Father was fine. Father would be home soon, I said. He just had to explain some things. She let me in, and I went to bed as planned.

Misinformation of that sort would continue to pacify her, day after day, year after year, until nearly the end of her life. At the end of her life, she would become combative and caustically witty, a sort of hick-town Voltaire, cynical and skeptical and so on. An autopsy would reveal several small tumors in her head, which doctors felt almost certainly accounted for this change in personality.

• • •

Father was sent to prison for two years, and he and Mother were sued successfully by George Metzger for everything they had—except for a few essential pieces of furniture and the crudely patched roof over their heads. All Mother's wealth, it turned out, was in Father's name.

Father did nothing effective to defend himself. Against all advice, he was his own lawyer. He pled guilty right after he was arrested, and he pled guilty again at the coroner's inquest, where he made no comment on what was evident to everyone—that he had very recently been beaten black and blue. Nor, as his own lawyer and mine, did he put on the record that any number of laws had been violated when I, only twelve years old, had been smeared with ink and exposed to public scorn.

The community was to be ashamed of nothing. Father was to be ashamed of everything. My father, the master of so many grand gestures and attitudes, turned out to be as collapsible as a paper cup. He had always known, evidently, that he wasn't worth a good God damn. He had only kept going, I think, because all that money, which could buy almost anything, kept coming in and coming in.

The shock to me wasn't that my father was so collapsible.

The shock to me was that Mother and I were so unsurprised.

Nothing had changed.

. . .

After we got home from the inquest, incidentally, which happened the day before Mrs. Metzger's funeral, we got a telephone call from my brother Felix at Fort Benning. Even before basic training had begun, he said, an officer had recommended that he be made an acting corporal, and that he go to Officers' Candidate School in thirteen weeks. This was because he had exhibited such leadership on the troop bus.

And I didn't talk, but I listened in on an extension.

Felix asked how everything was going with us, and neither Mother nor Father would tell him the truth.

Mother said to him, "You know us. We're just like Old Man River. We just keep rollin' along."

15

FATHER WAS defended by a lawyer in the lawsuit, but he was a jailbird by then. As things turned out, he would have been better off simply to hand over everything to George Metzger without a trial. At least he wouldn't have had to listen to proofs that he had admired Hitler, and that he had never done an honest day's work, and that he only pretended to be a painter, and that he had no education beyond high school, and that he had been arrested several times during his youth in other cities, and that he had regularly insulted his working relatives, and on and on.

There were enough ironies, certainly, to sink a battleship. The young lawyer who represented George Metzger had offered his services first to Father. He was Bernard Ketchum, and the Maritimo brothers had brought him to the coroner's inquest, urging Father to hire him and start using him then and there. He wasn't in the armed forces because he was blind in one eye. When he was little, a playmate had shot him in the eye with a beebee gun.

Ketchum was ruthless on Metzger's behalf, just as he

would have been ruthless with Metzger, if Father had hired him. He certainly never let the jury forget that Mrs. Metzger had been pregnant. He made the embryo a leading personality in town. It was always "she," since it was known to have been a female. And, although Ketchum himself had never seen her, he spoke familiarly of her perfectly formed little fingers and toes.

Years later, Felix and I would have reason to hire Ketchum, to sue the Nuclear Regulatory Commission and the Maritimo Brothers Construction Company and the Ohio Valley Ornamental Concrete Company for killing our mother with a radioactive mantelpiece.

That is how Felix and I got the money to buy this hotel, and old Ketchum is also a partner.

My instructions to Ketchum were these: "Don't forget to tell the jury about Mother's perfectly formed little fingers and toes."

. . .

After Father lost the lawsuit, we had to let all the servants go. There was no way to pay them, and Mary Hoobler and all the rest of them left in tears. Father was still in prison, so at least he was spared those wrenching farewells. Nor did he experience that spooky morning after, when Mother and I awoke in our separate rooms, and came out onto the balcony overhanging the main floor, and listened and sniffed.

Nothing was being cooked.

No one was straightening up the room below, and waiting for the time when she could make our beds.

This was new.

I of course got breakfast. It was easy and natural for me to do. And thus did I begin a life as a domestic servant to my mother and then to both my parents. As long as they lived, they never had to prepare a meal or wash a dish or make a bed or do the laundry or dust or vacuum or sweep, or shop for food. I did all that, and maintained a B average in school, as well.

What a good boy was I!

• • •

Eggs à la Rudy Waltz (age thirteen): Chop, cook, and drain two cups of spinach. Blend with two tablespoons of butter, a teaspoon of salt, and a pinch of nutmeg. Heat and put into three oven-proof bowls or cups.

Put a poached egg on top of each one, and sprinkle with grated cheese. Bake for five minutes at 375 degrees.

Serves three: the papa bear, the mama bear, and the baby bear who cooked it—and who will clean up afterwards.

• • •

As soon as the suit was settled, George Metzger took off for Florida with his two children. So far as I know, not one of them was ever seen in Midland City again. They had lived there a very short time, after all. Before they could put down roots, a bullet had come from nowhere for no reason, and drilled Mrs. Metzger between the eyes. And they hadn't made any friends to whom they would write year after year.

The two children, Eugene and Jane, in fact, found themselves as much outcasts as I was when we all returned to school. And we, in turn, were no worse off, socially, than the few children whose fathers or brothers had been killed in the war. We were all lepers, willy-nilly, for having shaken hands with Death.

We might as well have rung bells wherever we went, as lepers were often required to do in the Dark Ages.

Curious.

· · ·

Eugene and Jane were named, I found out only recently, for Eugene V. Debs, the labor hero from Terre Haute, Indiana, and Jane Addams, the Nobel prize–winning social reformer from Cedarville, Illinois. They were much younger than me, so we were in different schools. It was only recently, too, that I learned that they had found themselves as leprous as I was, and what had become of them in Florida, and on and on.

The source of all this information about the Metzgers has been, of course, their lawyer, who is now our lawyer, Bernard Ketchum.

Only at the age of fifty, thirty-eight years after I destroyed Mrs. Metzger's life, my life, and my parents' life with a bullet, have I asked anyone how the Metzgers were.

It was right here by the swimming pool at two in the morning. All the hotel guests were asleep, not that they are ever all that numerous. Felix and his new wife, his fifth wife, were there. Ketchum and his first and only wife were there. And I was there. Where was my mate? Who knows? I think I am a homosexual, but I can't be sure. I have never made love to anyone.

Nor have I tasted alcohol, except for homeopathic doses of it in certain recipes—but the others had been drinking champagne. Not since I was twelve, for that matter, have I swallowed coffee or tea, or taken a medicine, not even an aspirin or a laxative or an antacid or an antibiotic of any sort. This is an especially odd record for a person who is, as I am, a registered pharmacist, and who was the solitary employee on the night shift of Midland City's only all-night drugstore for years and years.

So be it.

I had just served the others and myself, as a surprise, *spuma di cioccolata,* which I had made the day before. There was one serving left over.

And we certainly all had plenty of things to think about, both privately and publicly, since our hometown had so recently been depopulated by the neutron bomb. We might so easily have had our peepholes closed, too, if we hadn't come down to take over the hotel.

When we heard about that fatal flash back home, in fact, I had quoted the words of William Cowper, which a sympathetic English teacher had given me to keep from killing myself when I was young:

God moves in a mysterious way
His wonders to perform;
He plants his footsteps in the sea,
And rides upon the storm.

So I said to Ketchum, after we had finished our chocolate seafoams, our *spume di cioccolata,* "Tell us about the Metzgers."

And Felix dropped his spoon. Curiosity about the Metzgers had been the most durable of all our family taboos. The taboo had surely existed in large measure for my own protection. Now I had broken it as casually as I had served dessert.

Old Ketchum was impressed, too. He shook his head wonderingly, and he said, "I never expected to hear a member of the Waltz family ask how any of the Metzgers were."

"I wondered out loud only once," said Felix, "—after I came home from the war. That was enough for me. I'd had a good time in the war, and I'd made a lot of contacts I could use afterwards, and I was pretty sure I was going to make a lot of money and become a big shot fast."

And he did become a big shot, of course. He eventually became president of NBC, with a penthouse and a limousine and all.

He also "tapped out early," as they say. After he was canned by NBC twelve years ago, when he was only forty-four, he couldn't find suitable work anywhere.

This hotel has been a godsend to Felix.

"So I was a citizen of the world when I came home," Felix went on. "Any city in any country, including my own hometown, was to me just another place where I might live or might not live. Who gave a damn? Anyplace you could put a microphone was home enough for me. So I treated my own mother and father and brother as natives of some poor, war-ravaged town I was passing through. They told me their troubles, as natives will, and I give them my absentminded sympathy. I cared some. I really did.

"I tried to look at the lighter side, as passers-through will, and I speculated as to what the formerly penniless Metzgers might be doing with their million dollars or so.

"And Mother, one of the most colorless women I would ever know, until she developed all those brain tumors toward the end," Felix went on, "—she slapped me. I was in uniform, but I hadn't been wounded or anything. I had just been a radio announcer.

"And then Father shouted at me, 'What the Metzgers do with their money is none of our business! It's theirs, do you hear me? I never want it mentioned again! We are poor people! Why should we break our hearts and addle our brains with rumors about the lives of millionaires?'"

• • •

According to Ketchum, George Metzger took his family to Florida because of a weekly newspaper which was for sale in Cedar Key, and because it was always warm down there, and because it was so far from Midland City. He bought the paper for a modest amount, and he invested the rest of the money in two thousand acres of open land near Orlando.

"A fool and his money can be a winning combination," said Ketchum of that investment made back in 1945. "That unprepossessing savannah, friends and neighbors, which George put in the name of his two children, and which they still own, became the magic carpet on which has been constructed the most successful family entertainment complex in human history, which is Walt Disney World."

There was water music throughout this conversation. We were far from the ocean, but a concrete dolphin expectorated lukewarm water into the swimming pool. The dolphin had come with the hotel, like the voodooist headwaiter, Hippolyte Paul De Mille. God only knows what the dolphin is connected to. God only knows what Hippolyte Paul De Mille is connected to.

He claims he can make a long-dead corpse stand up and walk around, if he wants it to.

I am skeptical.

"I surprise you," he says in Creole. "I show you someday."

• • •

George Metzger, according to Ketchum, is still alive, and a man of very modest means by choice—and still running a weekly paper in Cedar Key. He had kept enough money for himself, anyway, that he did not have to care whether anybody liked his paper or not. And very early on, in fact, he had lost most of his advertisers and subscribers to a new weekly, which did not share his exotic views on war and firearms and the brotherhood of man and so on.

So only his children were rich.

"Does anybody read his paper?" said Felix.

"No," said Ketchum.

"Did he ever remarry?" I said.

"No," said Ketchum.

Felix's fifth wife, Barbara, and the first loving wife he had ever had, in my opinion, found the solitude of old George Metzger in Cedar Key intolerable. She was a native of Midland City like the rest of us, and a product of its public schools. She was an X-ray technician. That was how Felix had met her. She had X-rayed his shoulder. She was only twenty-three. She was pregnant by Felix now, and so happy to be pregnant. She was such a true believer in how life could be enriched by children.

She was carrying Felix's first legitimate child. He had one illegitimate child, fathered in Paris during the war, and now in parts unknown. All his wives, though, had been very sophisticated about birth control.

And this lovely Barbara Waltz said of old George Metzger, "But he has those children, and they must adore him, and know what a hero he is."

"They haven't spoken to him for years," said Ketchum, with ill-concealed satisfaction. He plainly liked it when life went badly. That was comical to him.

Barbara was stricken. "Why?" she said.

Ketchum's own two children, for that matter, no

longer spoke to him, and had fled Midland City—and so had escaped the neutron bomb. They were sons. One had deserted to Sweden during the Vietnam War, and was working with alcoholics there. The other was a welder in Alaska who had flunked out of Harvard Law School, his father's alma mater.

"Your baby will be asking you that wonderful question soon enough," said Ketchum, as amused by his own bad luck as by anybody else's, "—'Why, why, why?' "

Eugene Debs Metzger, it turned out, lived in Athens, Greece, and owned several tankers, which flew the flag of Liberia.

His sister, Jane Addams Metzger, who found her mother dead and vacuum cleaner still running so long ago, a big, homely girl, as I recall, and big and homely still, according to Ketchum, was living with a refugee Czech playwright on Molokai, in the Hawaiian Islands, where she owned a ranch and was raising Arabian horses.

"She sent me a play by her lover," said Ketchum. "She thought maybe I could find a producer for it, since, of course, there in Midland City, Ohio, I was falling over producers every time I turned around."

And my brother Felix parodied the line about there being a broken heart for every light on Broadway in New York City. He substituted the name of Midland City's main drag. "There's a broken heart for every light on old Harrison Avenue," he said. And he got up, and went for more champagne.

His way up the stairs to the hotel proper was blocked

by a Haitian painter, who had fallen asleep while waiting for a tourist, any tourist, to come back from a night on the town. He had garish pictures of Adam and Eve and the serpent, and of Haitian village life, with all the people with their hands in their pockets, since the artist couldn't draw hands very well, and so on, lining the staircase on either side.

Felix did not disturb him. He stepped over him very respectfully. If Felix had seemed to kick him intentionally, Felix would have been in very serious trouble. This is no ordinary colonial situation down here. Haiti as a nation was born out of the only successful slave revolt in all of human history. Imagine that. In no other instance have slaves over-whelmed their masters, begun to govern themselves and to deal on their own with other nations, and repelled foreign-ers who felt that natural law required them to be slaves again.

So, as we had been warned when we bought the hotel here, any white or lightly colored person who struck or even menaced a Haitian in a manner suggesting a master-and-slave relationship would find himself in prison.

This was understandable.

• • •

While Felix was away, I asked Ketchum if the Czech refugee's play was any good. He said that he was in no position to judge, and that neither was Jane Metzger, since it was written in Czech. "It is a comedy, I'm told," he said. "It could be very funny."

"Funnier than my play, certainly," I said. And here is an eerie business: Twenty-three years ago, back in 1959, I entered a playwriting contest sponsored by the Caldwell Foundation, and I won, and my prize was a professional production of my play at the Theatre de Lys in Greenwich Village. It was called *Katmandu*. It was about John Fortune, Father's dairy farmer friend and then enemy, who is buried in Katmandu.

I stayed with my brother and his third wife, Genevieve. They lived in the Village, and I slept on their couch. Felix was only thirty-four, but he was already general manager of radio station WOR, and was about to head up the television department of Batten, Barton, Durstine & Osborn, the advertising agency. He was already having his clothes made in London.

And *Katmandu* opened and closed in a single night. This was my one fling away from Midland City, my one experience, until now, with inhabiting a place where I was not Deadeye Dick.

16

THE NEW YORK CITY critics found it hilarious that the author of *Katmandu* held a degree in pharmacy from Ohio State University. They found it obvious, too, that I had never seen India or Nepal, where half my play took place. How delicious they would have found it, if only they had known, that I had begun to write the play when I was only a junior in high school. How pathetic they would have found it, if only they had known, that I had been told that I should become a writer, that I had the divine spark, by a high school English teacher who had never been anywhere, either, who had never seen anything important, either, who had no sex life, either. And what a perfect name she had for a role like that: Naomi Shoup.

She took pity on me, and on herself, too, I'm sure. What awful lives we had! She was old and alone, and considered to be ridiculous for finding joy on a printed page. I was a social leper. I would have had no time for friends anyway. I went food shopping right after school, and started supper as soon as I got home. I did the laundry in the broken-down Maytag wringer-washer in the furnace room. I served supper to Mother and Father, and sometimes guests, and cleaned up afterwards. There would be dirty dishes from breakfast and lunch as well.

I did my homework until I couldn't keep my eyes open any longer, and then I collapsed into bed. I often slept in my clothing. And then I got up at six in the morning and did the ironing and vacuuming. And then I served breakfast to Mother and Father, and put a hot lunch for them in the oven. And then I made all the beds and I went to school.

"And what are your parents up to while you're doing all that housework?" Miss Shoup asked me. She had summoned me from a study hall, where I had been fast asleep, to a conference in her tiny office. There was a photograph of Edna St. Vincent Millay on her wall. She had to tell me who she was.

I was too embarrassed to tell old Miss Shoup the truth about what Mother and Father did with their time. They were zombies. They were in bathrobes and bedroom slippers all day long—unless company was expected. They stared into the distance a lot. Sometimes they would hug each other very lightly and sigh. They were the walking dead.

The next time Hippolyte Paul De Mille offers to raise a corpse for my amusement, I will say to him, "It is nothing I do not see yesterday."

· · ·

So I told Miss Shoup that Father did carpentry around the house, and of course painted and drew a lot, and ran a little antique business. The last time Father had touched any tools, in fact, was when he decapitated the house and smashed up his guns. I had never seen him paint or draw. His antique business consisted of trying to sell off what little was left of all the loot he had brought back from Europe in his glory days.

That was one way we went on eating—and heating. Another source of cash was a small legacy Mother received from a relative in Germany. She inherited it after the lawsuit was settled. Otherwise, the Metzgers would have got that, too. But most of our money came from Felix, who was extraordinarily generous without our ever asking him for anything.

And I told Miss Shoup that Mother gardened and helped me a lot with the housework, and helped Father with his antique business, and wrote letters to friends, and read a lot, and so on.

What Miss Shoup wanted to see me about, though, was an essay on this assigned subject: "The Midland City Person I Most Admire." My hero was John Fortune, who died in Katmandu when I was only six years old. She turned my ears crimson by saying that it was the finest piece of writing by a student that she had seen in forty years of teaching. She began to weep.

"You really must become a writer," she said. "And you must get out of this deadly town, too—as soon as you can.

"You must find what I should have had the courage to look for," she said, "what we should all have the courage to look for."

"What is that?" I said.

Her answer was this: "Your own Katmandu."

• • •

She had been watching me recently, she confessed. "You seem to be talking to yourself."

"Who else is there to talk to?" I said. "It's not talking anyway."

"Oh?" she said. "What is it?"

"Nothing," I said. I had never told anybody what it was, nor did I tell her. "It's just a nervous habit," I said. She would have liked it if I had told her all my secrets, but I never gave her that satisfaction.

It seemed safest and wisest to be as cold as ice to her, and to everyone.

But the answer to her question was this: I was singing to myself. It was scat singing, an invention of the black people. They had found it a good way to shoo the blues away, and so had I. "Booby dooby wop wop," I would sing to myself, and "Skaddy wee, skeedy wah," and so on. "Beedy op! Beedy op!"

And the miles went by, and the years went by. "Foodly yah, foodly yah. Zang reepa dop. Faaaaaaaaaaaaaaaaa!"

• • •

Linzer torte (from the *Bugle-Observer*): Mix half a cup of sugar with a cup of butter until fluffy. Beat in two egg yolks and half a teaspoon of grated lemon rind.

Sift a cup of flour together with a quarter teaspoon of salt, a teaspoon of cinnamon, and a quarter teaspoon of cloves. Add this to the sugar-and-butter mixture. Add one cup of unblanched almonds and one cup of toasted filberts, both chopped fine.

Roll out two-thirds of the dough until a quarter of an inch thick. Line the bottom and sides of an eight-inch pan with dough. Slather in a cup and a half of raspberry jam. Roll out the rest of the dough, make it into eight thin pencil shapes about ten inches long. Twist them a little, and lay them across the top in a decorative manner. Crimp the edges.

Bake in a preheated 350-degree oven for about an hour, and then cool at room temperature.

A great favorite in Vienna, Austria, before the First World War!

• • •

So I said nothing to my parents about wanting to become a writer until I had served a surprise dessert which I had gotten out of the paper, which was Linzer torte.

Father roused himself from living death sufficiently to say that the dessert took him back forty years. And, before he could sink out of sight again, I told him what Naomi Shoup had said to me.

"Half woman and half bird," he said.

125

"Sir?" I said.

"Miss Shoup," he said.

"I don't understand," I said.

"She is obviously a siren," he said. "A siren is half woman, half bird."

"I know what a siren is," I said.

"Then you know they lure sailors with their sweet songs to shipwrecks on rocks," he said.

"Yes, sir," I said. Since shooting Mrs. Metzger, I had taken to calling all grown men "sir." Like the secret scat singing, it somehow made my hard life just a trifle easier. I was a make-believe soldier of the lowest rank.

"What did Odysseus do in order to sail by the sirens safely?" he asked me.

"I forget," I said.

"He did what you must do now, whenever anybody tells you that you have an artistic gift of any kind," he said. "I only wish my father had told me what I tell you now."

"Sir?" I said.

"Plug your ears with wax, my boy—and lash yourself to the mast," he said.

• • •

"I wrote a thing about John Fortune, and she said it was good," I persisted. I did very little of that, I must say—persisting. During my time in the cage, all covered with ink, I concluded that the best thing for me and for those around me was to want nothing, to be enthusiastic about nothing, to be as unmotivated as possible, in fact, so that I would never again hurt anyone.

To put it another way: I wasn't to touch anything on this planet, man, woman, child, artifact, animal, vegetable, or mineral—since it was very likely to be connected to a push-pull detonator and an explosive charge.

And the fact that I had been working for the past month, late at night, on a major essay on a subject that excited me, was news to my parents. They never asked me what I might be doing at school.

School.

"John Fortune?" said Father. "What did you find to say about him?"

"I'll show you my essay," I said. Miss Shoup had given it back to me.

"No, no," said Father. "Just tell me." Now that I think about it, he may have been dyslectic. "I'd be interested to hear what you have to say about him, because I knew him well."

"I know," I said.

"Why didn't you ask me about him?" he said.

"I didn't want to bother you," I said. "You have so much to think about." I didn't say so, but I also knew that the loss of John Fortune as a friend, over Father's admiration of Hitler, was a painful subject for Father. I had caused him enough pain. I had caused everybody enough pain.

"He was a fool," said Father. "There is no wisdom to be found in Asia. It was that damn fool book that killed him."

"*Lost Horizon*—by James Hilton," I said. This was a very popular novel published in 1933, one year after my peephole opened. It told of a tiny, isolated country, a secret from the rest of the world, where no one ever tried to hurt anybody else, and where everybody was happy and nobody grew old. Hilton located this imaginary Garden of Eden somewhere in the Himalayas, and he called it "Shangri-La."

It was this book which inspired John Fortune to take off for the Himalayas after his wife died. It was possible back then for even an educated person, which Fortune wasn't, to suspect that contentment might be hidden somewhere on the map, like the treasure of Captain Kidd. Katmandu had certainly been visited by travelers often enough, but they all had to get there the way John Fortune got there, which was on a footpath from the Indian border—through mountains and jungle. A road wasn't put through until 1952, the year I graduated from pharmacy school.

And, my God, they've got a big airport there now. It can handle jets. My dentist, Herb Stacks, has been there three times so far, and his waiting room is chock-a-block with Nepalese art. That was how he and his family escaped the neutron bomb. They were in Katmandu at the time.

• • •

Father behaved as though I had pulled off a miracle of extrasensory perception, knowing about John Fortune and

Lost Horizon. "How could you possibly know that?" he said.

"I went through old newspapers at the public library," I said.

"Oh," he said. I don't think he had ever used the public library. "They keep old newspapers there?" he said with some surprise.

"Yes, sir," I said.

"Goodness—there must be a lot of them," he said. "Day after day, week after week." He asked me if people were in the library all the time, ". . . dredging up the past like that?" It may have seemed wrong to him that his own past in the newspaper hadn't been carted off to the dump. And I had come across a little of that, some of his letters to the editor in praise of Hitler.

"Well," he said, "—I certainly hope you never read that book."

"Lost Horizon?" I said. "I already have."

"You mustn't take it seriously," he said. "It's all bunk. This is as much Shangri-La as anywhere."

Now, at the age of fifty, I believe this to be true.

And, here in Haiti, I have begun to verbalize that sentiment, so intolerable to me when I was a teen-ager. We are going to have to go back to Midland City soon, at the pleasure of our government, to collect whatever personal property we want, and to file our claims against our government. It now seems certain: The entire county is to become a refugee center, possibly fenced.

KURT VONNEGUT

A dark thought: Perhaps the neutron bomb explosion wasn't so accidental after all.

In any event, and in anticipation of our brief return to our hometown, I have in conversation given Midland City this code name, which the Ketchums and my brother and his wife accept without protest: "Shangri-La."

17

THE NIGHT I told Father I wanted to be a writer, the night of the Linzer tortes, he ordered me to become a pharmacist instead, which I did. As Felix has pointed out, Father and Mother were understandably edgy about losing their last servant, among other things.

And Father made a ritual of lighting a cigar, and then he shook out the match and dropped it in what was left of the Linzer torte, and then he said again, "Be a pharmacist! Go with the grain of your heritage! There is no artistic talent in this family, nor will there ever be! You can imagine how much it hurts me to say so. We are business people, and that's all we can ever hope to be."

"Felix is gifted," I said.

"And so is every circus freak," said Father. "Yes—he has the deepest voice in the world, but have you ever listened to what he actually says when he's using his own mind, when some genuinely gifted person hasn't written something for him to say?"

I made no reply and he went on: "You and I and your mother and your brother are descended from solid, stolid, thick-skulled, unimaginative, unmusical, ungraceful German stock whose sole virtue is that it can never leave off working. You see in me a man who was flattered and lied to and coddled out of his proper destiny, which was a life in business, in rendering some sort of plodding but useful service to his community. Don't throw away your destiny the way I did. Be what you were born to be. Be a pharmacist!"

• • •

So I become a pharmacist. But I never gave up on being a writer, too, although I stopped talking about it. I cut poor old Naomi Shoup dead the next time she dared mention my divine spark to me. I told her that I had no wish to be distracted from my first love, which was pharmacy. Thus was I without a single friend in this world again.

I was permitted a certain number of electives when I enrolled as a pharmacy major at Ohio State. And, with nobody watching, so to speak, I took a course in playwriting in my sophomore year. I had by then heard of James Thurber, who had grown up right there in Columbus, and then gone on to New York City to write comically about the same sorts of people I had known in Midland City. And his biggest hit had been a play, *The Male Animal*.

"Scooby dooby do-wop! Deedly-ah! Deedly ah!" Maybe I could be like him.

So I turned my essay on John Fortune into a play.

• • •

Who was doing the housework back home meanwhile? I was still doing most of it. I wasn't your typical college boy, any more than I had been your typical high school boy. I still lived at home, but made the hundred-mile round-trip to Columbus three or four times a week, depending on what my schedule was.

I cut down on fancy cooking, I must say. I served an awful lot of canned stew in those days, and sometimes I didn't get around to serving it until midnight, either. Mother and Father groused a little bit, but not all that much.

Who was paying my tuition? My brother was.

• • •

I agree now that *Katmandu* was a ridiculous play. What made me keep working on it so long, even after I graduated and went to work as the night man at Schramm's Drugstore, were the lines at the very end. They so much deserved to be spoken in a theater. They weren't even my lines. They were the last words of John Fortune himself, which I found in an old *Bugle-Observer*.

The thing was this: He simply disappeared somewhere in Asia in 1938. He had sent postcards back from

San Francisco, and then Honolulu, and then Fiji, and then Manila, and Madras, and so on. But then the cards stopped. The very last one came from Agra, India, the site of the Taj Mahal.

One letter I found in the paper, published in 1939, long before anybody in Midland City found out what finally happened to Fortune, said this: "At least he saw the Taj Mahal."

But then, right at the end of World War Two, the *Bugle-Observer* got a letter from a British doctor who had been a prisoner of the Japanese for years and years. His name was David Brokenshire. It is easy for me to remember that, since he became a character in my play.

This Dr. Brokenshire had walked all alone on the footpath to Katmandu. He was studying folk medicine. So he had been in Nepal for about a year, when some natives brought to him a white man on a stretcher. The man had collapsed in front of the palace. He had just arrived, and he had double pneumonia. It was John Fortune, of course, and his costume was so strange to both the Englishman and the Nepalese that he was asked to say what it was. The answer was this: "Plain old, honest Ohio bib overalls."

So John Fortune's peephole closed and he was buried there in Katmandu, but not before he scrawled a message which Brokenshire promised to deliver sooner or later to the *Bugle-Observer* back in Midland City. But the doctor was in no hurry to get to the nearest mailbox. He went wandering into Tibet instead, and then northern Burma, and then China, where the Japanese captured him. They thought he was a spy. He didn't even know there was a war going on.

He wrote a book about it later. I read it. It is hard to find, but worth looking for. It is quite interesting.

But the point is that he didn't get to send John Fortune's last words, along with a map of where in Katmandu Fortune was buried, to Midland City until six years after Fortune's death. The words were these:

"To all my friends and enemies in the buckeye state. Come on over. There's room for everybody in Shangri-La."

18

$K_{ATMANDU}$, my contribution to Western civilization, has been performed three times before paying audiences—once at the Theatre de Lys in New York City in 1960, in the same month that Father died, and then twice on the stage of Fairchild High School in Midland City three years later. The female lead of the Midland City production was, incidentally, none other than Celia Hildreth Hoover, to whom Father had tried to present an apple so long ago.

In the first act of the play, which was set in Midland City, Celia, who in real life would eventually swallow Drāno, played the ghost of John Fortune's wife. In the second act, she was a mysterious Oriental woman he meets at the Taj Mahal. She offers to show him the way to Shangri-La, and leads the way over mountains and through jungle on the path to Katmandu. And then, after Fortune speaks his message for the people back in Midland City and dies, she doesn't say anything, but she reveals herself as the ghost of his wife again.

It isn't an easy part, and Celia had never done any acting at all before. She was only the wife of a Pontiac dealer, but I think she was actually at least as good as the professional actress who did it in New York City. She was certainly more beautiful. She hadn't yet been made all raddled and addled and snaggletoothed and haggard by amphetamine.

I forget the name of the actress in New York City now. I think maybe she dropped out of acting after *Katmandu*.

• • •

Speaking of amphetamine: Father's old friend Hitler was evidently one of the first people to experience its benefits. I read recently that his personal doctor kept him bright eyed and bushy tailed right up to the end with bigger and bigger doses of vitamins and amphetamine.

• • •

I went straight from pharmacy school to a job as all-night man at Schramm's Drugstore, six days a week from midnight to dawn. I still lived with my parents, but now I was able to make a substantial contribution to their support and my own. It was a dangerous job, since Schramm's, the only business establishment of any sort that was open all night, was a sort of lighthouse for lunatics and outlaws. My predecessor, old Malcolm Hyatt, who went to high school with my father, was killed by a robber from out of town. The robber swung off the Shepherdstown Turnpike, and closed old Hyatt's peephole with a sawed-off shotgun, and then swung back onto the Interstate again.

He was apprehended at the Indiana border, and tried and convicted, and sentenced to die over at Shepherdstown. They closed his peephole with electricity. In one microsecond he was hearing and seeing all sorts of things. In the next microsecond he was a wisp of undifferentiated nothingness again.

Served him right.

· · ·

The drugstore was owned by a man named Horton in Cincinnati, incidentally. There weren't any Schramms left in town. There used to be dozens of Schramms in town.

There used to be dozens of Waltzes in town, too. But when I went to work at Schramm's, there were only four of us—Mother, Father, and me, and my brother's first wife Donna. She was half of a set of what used to be identical twins. She and Felix were divorced, but she still called herself Donna Waltz. So she wasn't a real Waltz, a blood Waltz.

And she would never have been a Waltz of any sort, if Felix hadn't accidentally put her through a windshield the day after he was discharged from the Army. He hardly knew her, since her family had moved to Midland City from Kokomo, Indiana, while he was at war. He couldn't even tell her from her twin, Dina.

They were out joyriding in her father's car. Thank God it wasn't our car, anyway. We didn't have a car anymore. We didn't have shit anymore, and Father was still in prison. But Felix was driving. He was at the wheel. And the brakes locked. It was a prewar Hudson. There weren't any postwar cars yet.

So Donna went through the windshield, and she didn't look anything like her sister anymore. And Felix married her after she got out of the hospital. She was only eighteen years old, but she had a full set of false teeth, uppers and lowers.

Felix now refers to his first marriage as a "shotgun wedding." Her relatives and friends felt it was his duty to marry her, whether he loved her or not—and Felix says that he felt that way, too. Usually, when people talk about shotgun weddings, they have pregnancy in mind. A man has impregnated a woman, so he has to marry her.

Felix didn't get his first wife pregnant before he married her, but he put her through a windshield. "I might as well have got her pregnant," he said the other night. "Putting her through a windshield came to very much the same sort of thing."

• • •

Very early on at Schramm's, long before I ran off to New York City to see my play produced, a drunk came in at about two A.M., maybe, and he squinted at the sign on the prescription counter which said, RUDOLPH WALTZ, R.PH.

He evidently knew something of our family's distinguished history, although I don't think we had ever met before. And he was drunk enough to say to me, "Are you the one who shot the woman, or are you the one who put the woman through the windshield?"

He wanted a chocolate malted milkshake, I remember. Schramm's hadn't had a soda fountain for at least five years. He wanted one anyway. "You just give me a little milk and ice cream and chocolate syrup, and I'll make it myself," he said. And then he fell down.

• • •

He didn't call me "Deadeye Dick." Very rarely did anybody do that to my face. But my nickname was said often enough behind my back in all sorts of crowds—in stores, at movies, in eating places. Or maybe somebody would shout it at me from a passing car. It was a thing for drunks or young people to do. No mature and respectable person ever called me "Deadeye Dick."

But one unsettling aspect of the all-night job at Schramm's, one I hadn't anticipated, was the telephone there. Hardly a night passed that some young person, feeling wonderfully daring and witty, no doubt, would telephone to ask me if I was Deadeye Dick.

I always was. I always will be.

• • •

There was plenty of time for reading on the job, and there were any number of magazines on the racks. And most of the business I did at night wasn't at all complicated, didn't have anything to do with pharmacy. Mainly, I sold cigarettes and, surprisingly, watches and the most expensive perfumes. The watches and perfumes were presents, of course, for birthdays and anniversaries which were remembered only after every other store in town had closed.

So I was reading *Writer's Digest* one night, and I came across an announcement of the Caldwell Foundation's contest for playwrights. The next thing I knew, I was back in the stock room, pecking away on the rattletrap Corona portable typewriter we used for making labels. I was writing a new draft of *Katmandu*.

And I won first prize.

. . .

Sauerbraten à la Rudolph Waltz, R.Ph.: Mix in a saucepan a cup of wine vinegar, half a cup of white wine, half a cup of cider vinegar, two sliced onions, two sliced carrots, a rib of celery, chopped, two bay leaves, six whole allspice, crushed, two cloves, two tablespoons of crushed peppercorns, and a tablespoon of salt. Bring just to a boil.

Pour it hot over a four-pound rump roast, rolled and tied, in a deep bowl. Turn the meat around and around in the mixture. Cover the bowl and refrigerate for three days. Turn the meat in the mixture several times a day.

Take the meat out of the marinade and dry it. Sear it on all sides in eight tablespoons of beef drippings in a braising pan. When it is nicely browned, take it out of the pan and pour out the drippings. Put the meat back in the pan, heat up the marinade, and pour it over the meat. Simmer for about three hours. Pour off the liquid, strain, and remove the excess fat. Keep the meat hot in the braising pan.

Melt three tablespoons of butter in a saucepan, and blend in three tablespoons of flour and a tablespoon of sugar. Gradually pour in the marinade, and stir until you have a uniform sauce. Add one cup of crushed gingersnaps, and simmer the sauce for about six minutes.

That's it!

• • •

For three days I did not tell Mother and Father that I had won the contest. It takes that long to make sauerbraten. The sauerbraten was a complete surprise, since Mother and Father never went into the kitchen. They simply waited at the table like good little children, to see what was going to come out of there.

When they had eaten all the sauerbraten they wanted, and said again and again how good it was, I spoke as follows to them: "I am now twenty-seven years old. I have been cooking for you for twelve years now, and I have enjoyed every minute of it. But now I have won a playwriting contest, and my play is going to be produced professionally in New York City three months from now. I will of course have to be there for six weeks of rehearsals.

"Felix says I can stay with him and Genevieve," I went on. "I will sleep on their couch. Their apartment is only three blocks from the theater." Genevieve, incidentally, is the wife Felix now refers to as "Anyface." She had almost no eyebrows, and very thin lips, so that, if she wanted anything memorable in the way of features, she had to paint them on.

I told Mother and Father that I had hired Cynthia Hoobler, the daughter-in-law of our old cook Mary Hoobler, to come in and care for them while I was gone. I would pay her from money I had saved.

I expected no trouble, since the servant problem was all taken care of, and got none. These people, after all, were like characters at the end of a novel or a play, who have been wrong about all sorts of things throughout the action, and finally something has settled their hash.

Mother spoke first. "Goodness," she said. "Good luck."

"Yes," said Father. "Good luck."

Little did I dream that Father had only a few more months to live then.

19

TIME FLEW. In a twinkling I was on Christopher Street in Greenwich Village at high noon, gazing up at a theater marquee as snowflakes kissed my face. It was February 14, 1960. My father was still in good health, as far as I knew. The words on the marquee were these:

KATMANDU

A NEW DRAMA

BY RUDY WALTZ

Rehearsals were over. We would open that night.

Father had had his studio, with its dusty skylight and nude model in Vienna, where he had found out he couldn't paint. Now I had my name up on a theater marquee in New York City, where I had found out I couldn't write. The play was a catastrophe. The more the poor actors rehearsed it, the more stupid and depressing it became.

The actors and the director, and the representatives of

the Caldwell Foundation, which would never sponsor another play contest, had stopped speaking to me. I was barred from the theater. It wasn't that I had made impossible demands. My offense was that I seemed to know less about the play than anybody. I simply was not worth talking to.

If I was asked about this line or that one, it was as though I had never heard it before. I was likely to say something like "My goodness—I wonder what I meant by that."

Nor did I seem at all interested in rediscovering why I had said this or that.

The thing was this: I was startled not to be Deadeye Dick anymore. Suddenly nobody knew that I was remarkable for having shot and killed a pregnant woman. I felt like a gas which had been confined in a labeled bottle for years, and which had now been released into the atmosphere.

I no longer cooked. It was Deadeye Dick who was always trying to nourish back to health those he had injured so horribly.

I no longer cared about the play. It was Deadeye Dick, tormented by guilt in Midland City, who had found old John Fortune's quite pointless death in Katmandu, as far away from his hometown as possible, somehow magnificent. He himself yearned for distance and death.

So, there in Greenwich Village, looking up at my name on the marquee, I was nobody. My braincase might as well have been filled with stale ginger ale.

Thus, when the actors were still talking to me, could

I have had a conversation like this with poor Sheldon Woodcock, the actor who was playing John Fortune:

"You've got to help me get a handle on this part," he said.

"You're doing fine," I said.

"I don't feel like I'm doing fine," he said. "The guy is so inarticulate."

"He's a simple farmer," I said.

"That's just it—he's too simple," he said. "I keep thinking he has to be an idiot, but he isn't an idiot, right?"

"Anything but," I said.

"He never says why he wants to get to Katmandu," he said. "All these people either try to help him get to Katmandu or keep him from getting to Katmandu, and I keep thinking, 'Why the hell should anybody care whether he gets to Katmandu or not?' Why not Tierra del Fuego? Why not Dubuque? He's such a lunk, does it make any difference where he is?"

"He's looking for Shangri-La," I said. "He says that many times—that he wants to find Shangri-La."

"Thirty-four times," he said.

"I beg your pardon?" I said.

"He says that thirty-four times: 'I am looking for Shangri-La.'"

"You counted?" I said.

"I thought somebody better," he said. "That's a lot of times to say anything in just two hours—especially if the person who says it says practically nothing else."

"Cut some of them, if you want," I said.

"Which ones?" he said.

"Whichever ones seem excessive to you," I said.

"And what do I say instead?" he said.

"What would you like to say?" I said.

So he swore under his breath, but then he pulled himself together. I would be barred from the theater soon after this. "Maybe you don't realize this," he said with bitter patience, "but actors don't make up what they say on the stage. They look like they've made it up, if they're any good, but actually a person called a 'playwright' has first written down every word."

"Then just say what I've written," I said. The secret message in this advice was that I was so light-headed, being away from home for the first time in my life, that I didn't care what happened next. The play was going to be a big flop, but nobody in New York knew what I looked like anyway. I wasn't going to be arrested. I wasn't going to be displayed in a cage, all covered with ink.

I wasn't going home again, either. I would get a job as a pharmacist somewhere in New York. Pharmacists can always find work. And I would do what my brother Felix did—send money home. And then, step by step, I would experiment with having a home of my own and a life of my own, maybe try pairing off with this kind of person or that one, to see how that went.

"Tell me again about my great death scene in the arms of Dr. Brokenshire in Katmandu, with the sitar music," said Woodcock.

"Okay," I said.

"I think I'm in Shangri-La," he said.

"That's right," I said.

"And I know I'm dying," he said. "I don't just think I'm sick, and I'm going to get better again."

"The doctor makes it clear you're dying," I said.

"Then how can I believe I'm in Shangri-La?" he said.

"Pardon me?" I said.

"Another thing I say all through the play," he said, "is that nobody dies in Shangri-La. But here I'm dying, so how can I be in Shangri-La?"

"I'll have to think about it," I said.

"You mean this is the first time you've thought about it?" he said.

And on and on like that.

"Seventeen times," he said.

"Pardon me?" I said.

"Seventeen times I say that nobody dies in Shangri-La."

• • •

So, with opening night only a few hours away, I dawdled from the theater to my brother's duplex apartment, three blocks away. The snowflakes were few, and they melted when they landed. I had given up reading or listening to news since I had come to New York, and so did not know that the Ice Age was reclaiming southwestern Ohio with the most terrible blizzard in history there.

At just about the time the curtain went up on *Katmandu,* that blizzard would come busting in the back door of the old carriage house back home, and then it would fling open the great front portals from the inside, just as Father had done for Celia Hildreth so long ago.

People talk a lot about all the homosexuals there are to see in Greenwich Village, but it was all the neuters that caught my eye that day. These were my people—as used as I was to wanting love from nowhere, as certain as I was that almost anything desirable was likely to be booby-trapped.

I had a fairly funny idea. Someday all we neuters would come out of our closets and form a parade. I even decided what banner our front rank should carry, as wide as Fifth Avenue. A single word would be printed on it in letters four feet high:

EGREGIOUS.

Most people think that word means terrible or unheard of or unforgivable. It has a much more interesting story than that to tell. It means "outside the herd."

Imagine that—thousands of people, outside the herd.

•   •   •

I let myself into Felix's duplex. The place was faintly reminiscent of our childhood home, since the master bedroom was upstairs, and opened onto a balcony that overhung the living-dining room. Felix and I had already rearranged some of the furniture—to better accommodate the party we would be giving after the show. Caterers would bring the food. As I say, I didn't give a damn about food anymore.

And nobody in his right mind was going to come to the party anyway.

It wasn't my party anyway, any more than it was my stupid play. I had regressed to being the boy I used to be—before I shot Mrs. Metzger. I was barely twelve years old.

I supposed that I would have the place to myself all afternoon. Felix and his wife Genevieve, "Anyface," were at radio station WOR, I thought. She still had her job as a receptionist there, and Felix was cleaning out his desk there, preparing to move on to bigger things at Batten, Barton, Durstine & Osborn.

They, in turn, had every reason to assume that I would be at the theater, making last-minute changes in the play. I had not told them that I had been barred from there.

So I wandered up on the balcony, and I sat on a hard-backed chair there. It must have been something I used to do in the carriage house when I was genuinely innocent and twelve years old—to sit very still on the balcony, and to appreciate every sound that floated up to me. It wasn't eavesdropping. It was music appreciation.

And thus it was that I overheard the final dissolution of my brother's second marriage, and some unkind character sketches of Felix and myself and our parents and Genevieve, and some others I did not know. Genevieve came bursting into the apartment first, so angry that she was spitting like a cat, and then, half a minute later, Felix entered. She had come in one cab, and he had chased her in another. And down below me, and out of my line of sight, an acrimonious, atonal duet for viola and string bass was improvised. They both had such noble voices. She was the viola, and he was the bass.

Or maybe it was a comedy. Maybe it is amusing when physically attractive, well-to-do great apes in an urban setting hate each other so much:

DUPLEX

A NEW COMEDY
BY RUDY WALTZ.

The curtain rises on a Greenwich Village duplex, severely modern, expensive, white. There are fresh flowers. There is fresh fruit. There is impressive electronic apparatus for reproducing music. GENEVIEVE WALTZ, a beautiful young woman whose features must be painted on like those of a China doll, enters through the front door, terminally furious. Her young and successful husband, FELIX, wearing clothes made in London, follows almost at once. He is just as mad. On the balcony sits RUDY WALTZ, a neutered pharmacist from Ohio, FELIX'S kid brother. He is large and good-looking, but is so sexless and shy that he might as well be made out of canned tuna fish. Incredibly, he has written a play which is going to open in a few hours. He knows it is no good. He considers himself a big mistake. He considers life a big mistake. It probably shouldn't be going on. It is all he can do to give life the benefit of the doubt. There is a frightful secret in his past, which he and his brother have withheld from GENEVIEVE, that he is a murderer. All three are products of public school systems in the

Middle West, although GENEVIEVE *now sounds vaguely British, and* FELIX *sounds like a Harvard-educated secretary of state. Only* RUDY *is still a twanging hick.*

GENEVIEVE: Leave me alone. Go back to work.

FELIX: I'll help you pack.

GENEVIEVE: I can pack all right.

FELIX: Can you kick your own butt as you go out the door?

GENEVIEVE: You're sick. You're from a very sick family. Thank God we never had a child.

FELIX: There was a young man from Dundee, Who buggered an ape in a tree. The results were most horrid, All ass and no forehead, Three balls and a purple goatee.

GENEVIEVE: I didn't know your father was from Dundee. *(She opens a closet)* Look at all the pretty suitcases in here.

FELIX: Fill 'em up. I want every trace of you out of here.

GENEVIEVE: Some of my perfume may have gotten into the draperies. You should probably burn them in the fireplace.

FELIX: Just pack, baby. Just pack.

GENEVIEVE: It's my house as much as it's your house. That's just a theory, of course.

FELIX: I'll pay you off. I'll buy you out.

GENEVIEVE: And I'll give your brother my clothes. He can have all my stuff here. I don't even have to pack. I'll just walk out of here, and start out new.

FELIX: What is that supposed to mean?

GENEVIEVE: Starting out new? Well, you go to Bendel's or Saks or Bloomingdale's, naked except for a credit card—

FELIX: My brother and your clothes.

GENEVIEVE: I think he would enjoy being a woman. I think that's what he was meant to be. That would be nice for you, too, since then you could marry him. I want you to be happy, as hard as that may be for you to believe.

FELIX: That is the end.

GENEVIEVE: We passed that long ago.

FELIX: That is the *very* end.

GENEVIEVE: And the very, very end is coming up. Just get out of here and let me pack.

FELIX: I am to have no feelings of loyalty toward members of my own family?

GENEVIEVE: I was part of your family. Don't you remember that ceremony we went through at City Hall? You probably thought it was an opera, where you were supposed to sing, "I do." If you're from such a close-knit family, why weren't any of its members there?

FELIX: You were in such a hurry to get married.

GENEVIEVE: Was I? I guess I was. I was glad to get married. There was going to be so much happiness. And there was happiness, too, wasn't there?

FELIX: Some. Sure.

GENEVIEVE: Until your brother came along.

FELIX: It's not his fault.

GENEVIEVE: It's your fault.

FELIX: Tell me how.

GENEVIEVE: The very, very end is coming up now. Are you sure you want to hear it?

FELIX: How is it my fault?

GENEVIEVE: You are so ashamed of him. You must be ashamed of your parents, too. Otherwise, why have I never met them?

FELIX: They're too sick to leave home.

GENEVIEVE: And we, with an income of over one hundred thousand dollars a year, have been too poor to visit them. Are they dead?

FELIX: No.

GENEVIEVE: Are they in a crazy house?

FELIX: No.

GENEVIEVE: I'm very good at visiting people in crazy houses. My own mother was in a crazy house when I was in high school, and I visited her. She was wonderful. I was wonderful. I told you my mother was in the crazy house for a while.

FELIX: Yes.

GENEVIEVE: I thought you should know—in case we wanted a baby. It isn't anything to be ashamed of, anyway. Or is it?

FELIX: Nothing to be ashamed of.

GENEVIEVE: So tell me the worst about your parents.

FELIX: Nothing.

GENEVIEVE: Then I'll tell you what's wrong with them. They're not good enough for you. You deserve something far more classy. What a snob you are.

FELIX: It's more complicated.

GENEVIEVE: I doubt it. I can't remember anything about you that was the least bit complicated. Making a good impression at all costs—that accounted for everything.

FELIX: There's a little more to me than that, thank you.

GENEVIEVE: No. There was nothing to you but urbane perfection, until your brother arrived—and turned out to be a circus freak.

FELIX: Don't you call him that.

GENEVIEVE: I'm telling you what you think of him. And what was my duty as a wife? To protect your perfection as much as possible: To pretend that there was absolutely nothing wrong with him. At least I never cringed. You did all the cringing.

FELIX: Cringing?

GENEVIEVE: With your head in your hands, whenever he's around. You could die of shame. You think he hasn't noticed that? You think he hasn't noticed that we're all set up for entertaining, but we somehow never have people in?

FELIX: I've been protecting him.

GENEVIEVE: Protecting you, you mean. This lovely fight we've had—it wasn't about anything I said to him. I've been very nice to him. It was what I said to you that you couldn't stand.

FELIX: With a million people listening.

GENEVIEVE: Five other people in the reception room. And not one heard what I said—because I whispered it to you. But people as far as Chicago must have heard what you yelled back at me. I was actually happily married this morning—for a few seconds—before you yelled at me. I was feeling very pretty and cherished as I sat at the reception desk. We had made love this morning, as you may remember. You had better burn the bottom sheet—along with the draperies. There were five strangers in the reception room, imagining, I think, what sort of life and lover I must have to be so impish and gay—so early in the morning. Into the reception room comes a young broadcasting executive, flawlessly groomed, urbane and sexy. What marvelous New York bullshit! He is the lover! He stops and kisses her, and then she whispers in his ear. It was almost as though New York City were true. A couple of spunky kids from the Middle West, making it big in Gotham.

FELIX: You shouldn't have whispered what you did.

GENEVIEVE: I'll say it again: "Tell your brother to take a bath."

FELIX: What a time to say a thing like that.

GENEVIEVE: His play is opening tonight, and he stinks to high heaven. He hasn't taken a bath since he's been here.

FELIX: You call a remark like that romantic?

GENEVIEVE: I call it family life. I call it intimacy. That's all over now. *(She hauls a suitcase from the closet, opens it, flops it gaping on the couch)* Look how hungry that suitcase is.

FELIX: I'm sorry I said what I said.

GENEVIEVE: You yelled. You yelled, "Shut the fuck up!" You yelled, "If you don't like my relatives, get the hell out of my life!"

FELIX: It was over in a minute.

GENEVIEVE: You bet your English boots it was. And I walked out of that office, never to return. I'm gone, old friend. What a bore and a boor you were to follow me. What a hick.

(The closet contains mostly sporting goods, ski parkas, wetsuits, warm-up jackets, and so on. GENEVIEVE sorts through these, throwing what she wants on the couch, near the open suitcase. FELIX'S manly bumptiousness decays as he watches. He is a person of weak character, an actor who can't bear to be ignored. He elects to recapture GENEVIEVE'S attention by becoming pitiful and harrowingly frank.)

FELIX *(loudly abject):* It's true, it's true, it's true.

GENEVIEVE *(uninterested):* We never did go scuba diving.

FELIX: I *am* ashamed of my family! You're right! You got me!

(RUDY doesn't do anything through all this. He just sits.)

GENEVIEVE: Scuba was next.

FELIX: Father served a prison term, if you want to know.

GENEVIEVE *(unexpectedly fascinated):* Really?

FELIX: Now you know.

GENEVIEVE: What for?

(Pause.)

FELIX: Murder.

GENEVIEVE *(moved):* Oh, my God. How awful.

FELIX: Now you know. There's a nice piece of gossip for the broadcast industry.

GENEVIEVE: Never mind the gossip. What it must have done to your brother—what it must have done to you.

FELIX: I'm all right.

GENEVIEVE: There's no reason why you should be. And your poor brother—no wonder he is the way he is. I thought he had been born defective, that the umbilical cord had strangled him or something. I thought he was an idiot savant.

FELIX: What's an idiot savant?

GENEVIEVE: Somebody who's stupid in every possible way but one—like playing the piano.

FELIX: He can't play the piano.

GENEVIEVE: But he wrote a play—and it's going to be produced. He may not take baths. He may not have any friends. He may be so shy he's afraid to talk to anybody. But he wrote a play, and he has an extraordinary vocabulary. He has a bigger vocabulary than both of us put together, and sometimes he says something that is really very funny or wise.

FELIX: He has a degree in pharmacy.

GENEVIEVE: I thought he was an idiot savant in that way, too—theater and pharmacy. But he's the son of a murderer. No wonder he's the way he is. No wonder he wants to be invisible. I saw him walking down Christopher Street last Sunday, and he was as big and handsome as Gary Cooper, but nobody else could see him. He went into a coffee shop, and sat down at the counter, but he couldn't get waited on—because he wasn't there. No wonder.

FELIX: Don't ask for details of the murder.

(Pause.)

GENEVIEVE: That's a request I'm bound to honor. Is he in prison now?

FELIX: No—but he might as well be. He might as well be dead.

GENEVIEVE: Everything stops—as I suddenly understand.

FELIX: Please stay, Gen. I don't want to be one of those jerks who gets married and divorced, married and divorced, married and divorced again. Something's very wrong with them.

GENEVIEVE: I can't ever go back to the radio station again—not after that scene. It was so embarrassing.

FELIX: I don't want you to work anymore anyway.

GENEVIEVE: I enjoy work. I enjoy having money of my own. What would I do—sit around the house all day?

FELIX: Have a baby.

GENEVIEVE: Oh, my goodness.

FELIX: Why not?

GENEVIEVE: Do you really think I would make a good
    mother?

FELIX: The best.

GENEVIEVE: What would you want—a boy or a girl?

FELIX: Either one. Whatever it was, I'd love it.

GENEVIEVE: Oh, my, oh, my. I think I'm going to cry
    now.

FELIX: Just don't walk out on me. I love you so.

GENEVIEVE: I won't.

FELIX: Do you believe I love you?

GENEVIEVE: I'd better, I guess.

FELIX: I'm going back to the office. I'll clean out my desk.
    I'll apologize to everybody for the scene I made. It
    was all my fault. My brother does stink. He should
    take a bath, and I thank you for saying so. Promise me
    you'll be here when I get back.

GENEVIEVE: Promise.

(FELIX *exits through the front door.* GENEVIEVE *starts putting
things back in the closet.*)

RUDY: Ahem.

GENEVIEVE: Hello?

RUDY: Ahem.

GENEVIEVE *(scared):* Who's up there, please?

RUDY *(standing, showing himself):* It's me.

GENEVIEVE: Oh, my.

RUDY: I didn't want to scare you.

GENEVIEVE: You heard all that.

RUDY: I didn't want to interrupt.

GENEVIEVE: We don't believe half of what we said.

RUDY: It's all right. I was going to take a bath anyway.

GENEVIEVE: You don't even have to.

RUDY: The house back home is so cold in the winter. You get out of the habit of taking baths. We all get used to the way we smell.

GENEVIEVE: I'm so sorry you heard.

RUDY: It's okay. I don't have any more feelings than a rubber ball. You said how nobody sees me, how I never can get waited on . . . ?

GENEVIEVE: You heard that, too.

RUDY: That's because I'm a neuter. I'm no sex. I'm out of the sex game entirely. Nobody knows how many neuters there are, because they're invisible to most people. I'll tell you something, though: There are millions in this town. They should have a parade sometime, with big signs saying, TRIED SEX ONCE, THOUGHT IT WAS STUPID, NO SEX FOR TEN YEARS, FEEL WONDERFUL, FOR ONCE IN YOUR LIFE, THINK ABOUT SOMETHING BESIDES SEX.

GENEVIEVE: You really can be funny sometimes.

RUDY: Idiot savant. No good at life, but very funny sometimes with the commentary.

GENEVIEVE: I'm sorry about your father.

RUDY: He never murdered anybody.

GENEVIEVE: He didn't?

RUDY: He wouldn't hurt a fly. But he was still a very bad father to have. Felix and I stopped bringing friends home, because he was so embarrassing. He wasn't anything and he never did anything, but he still thought he was so important. He was very spoiled as a child, I guess. We used to get him to help us with our homework, and then we'd get to school and find out that everything he said was wrong. You know what happens if you give a raccoon a lump of sugar?

GENEVIEVE: No.

RUDY: Raccoons always wash their food before they eat it.

GENEVIEVE: I've heard that. Back in Wisconsin, we had raccoons.

RUDY: A raccoon will take a lump of sugar down to the water, and wash it and wash it and wash it.

(Pause.)

GENEVIEVE: Aha! Until the sugar's gone.

RUDY: And that's what growing up was like for Felix and me. We had no father when we got through. Mother still thinks he's the greatest man in the world.

GENEVIEVE: But you still love your parents anyway.

RUDY: Neuters don't love anybody. They don't hate anybody either.

GENEVIEVE: But you've been keeping house for your parents for years and years, haven't you? Or isn't that true?

RUDY: Neuters make very good servants. They're not your great seekers of respect, and they usually cook pretty well.

GENEVIEVE *(feeling creepy):* You're a very strange person,
Rudy Waltz.

RUDY: That's because *I'm* the murderer.

GENEVIEVE: WHAT?

RUDY: There's a murderer in the family, all right—but it
isn't Father. It's me.

(Pause.)

(Curtain.)

• • •

Thus did I prevent my brother's fathering a child
back then. Genevieve cleared out of the duplex, not wishing to be there alone with a murderer, and she and Felix
never got together again. The child they had talked about
having would be twenty-two years old now. The child
Eloise Metzger was carrying when I shot her would be
thirty-eight! Think of that.

Who knows what those people would be doing now,
instead of drifting around nowhere, mere wisps of undifferentiated nothingness. They could be so busy now.

• • •

To this day, I have never told Felix about how I overheard his conversation with Genevieve from the balcony,
and about how I scared her out of the duplex, never to
return. I wrecked the marriage. It was an accident-prone

time in my life, just as it was an accident-prone time in my life when I shot Mrs. Metzger.

That's all I can say.

. . .

I had to let my sister-in-law know that I was somebody to be reckoned with—that I was a murderer. That was my claim to fame.

20

THE MORNING AFTER *Katmandu* opened and closed, Felix and I were flying over a landscape as white and blank as our lives. Felix had lost his second wife. I was the laughingstock of New York. We were in a six-passenger private plane, traversing a southwestern Ohio which appeared to be as lifeless as a polar ice cap. Somewhere down there was Midland City. The power was off. The phone lines were out.

How could anyone still be alive down there?

The sky was clear, anyway, and the air was still. The blizzard which had done this was now raging somewhere off Labrador.

. . .

Felix and I were in a plane which belonged to Barrytron, Ltd., a manufacturer of sophisticated weapons systems, the largest single employer in Midland City. With us were Fred T. Barry, the founder and sole owner of Barrytron, and his mother, Mildred, and their pilot.

Mr. Barry was a bachelor and his mother was a widow, and they were tireless globe-trotters. Felix and I learned from their conversation that they had been to cultural events all over the planet—arm-in-arm at film festivals and premiers of new ballets and operas, at openings of museum shows, and on and on. And I would be the last to mock them for being such frivolous gadabouts, since it was my play which had brought them and their airplane to New York City. They did not know me or Felix, nor had they more than a nodding acquaintance with our parents. But they had found it imperative that they be at the opening of the only full-length play by a citizen of Midland City which had ever been produced commercially.

How could I not like them for that?

What is more: This mother-and-son team had stayed to the very end of *Katmandu*. Only twenty people did that, including Felix and me. I know. I counted the house. And the Barrys clapped and whistled and stamped as the curtain came down. They were so uninhibited. And Mrs. Barry could certainly whistle. She had been born in England, and in her youth she had been an imitator in music halls of various birds of the British Empire.

· · ·

Mr. Barry thought a lot more of his mother than I thought of mine. After his mother died, he would try to immortalize her by having the Maritimo Brothers Construction Company build an arts center on stilts in Sugar Creek, and naming it in her honor.

My own mother effectively wrecked that scheme, persuading the community that the arts center and its contents were monstrosities. After that came the neutron bomb. There is nobody left in Midland City anymore to know or care who Mildred Barry might have been.

The scheme for turning the empty husks of my town into housing for refugees moves forward apace, incidentally. The President himself has called it "a golden opportunity."

Bernard Ketchum, our resident shyster here at the Grand Hotel Oloffson, says that Haitian refugees should follow the precedent set by white people, and simply discover Florida or Virginia or Massachusetts or whatever. They could come ashore, and start converting people to voodooism.

"It's a widely accepted principle," he says, "that you can claim a piece of land which has been inhabited for tens of thousands of years, if only you will repeat this mantra endlessly: 'We discovered it, we discovered it, we discovered it. . . .' "

• • •

Fred Barry's mother Mildred had an English accent which she had done nothing to modify, although she had lived in Midland City for a quarter of a century or more.

Her black servants, I know, were very fond of her. She knew exactly what kind of a fool she was, and she loved to keep her servants laughing at her all the time.

There in that little plane, she imitated the bulbul of

Malaysia and the morepork owl of New Zealand, and so on. I identified a basic mistake my parents had made about life: They thought that it would be very wrong if anybody ever laughed at them.

• • •

I keep wanting to say that Fred T. Barry was the grandest neuter I ever saw. He certainly had no sex life. He didn't even have friends. It was all right with him if life ended at any time, obviously, since this was a suicidal flight we were on. He didn't care much if I died, either, or Felix or his mother—or the pilot, who had gone to high school with my brother, and who was scared stiff. If we had an engine failure before we reached Cincinnati, the nearest open runway, where could we land?

But the satisfaction Mr. Barry found in the company of his mother and in their harum-scarum visits to athletic and cultural events all over the world was anything but proof of neutrality. If he liked any part of life that much, he couldn't march in the great parade of neuters in the sweet by-and-by.

Or his mother, either.

• • •

Fred and his mother really had liked *Katmandu,* and they had stayed up late afterwards, so they could get early editions of the morning newspapers and read the reviews. One of the things that made them really mad was that none of the critics had stayed long enough to find out whether John Fortune had found Shangri-La or not.

Mr. Barry said that he would like to see the play performed sometime with an all-Ohio cast. He said that he didn't think New York actors could fully appreciate why it might be important for a simple farmer to die on a quest for wisdom in Asia, even if there wasn't all that much wisdom to find over there.

And that would actually come to pass in three years, as I've said: The Midland County Mask and Wig Club would revive *Katmandu* on the high school stage, and they would give the female lead to poor Celia Hoover.

Oh, my.

· · ·

I keep calling Fred T. Barry "Mr. Barry," as though he were older than God. My goodness, he was only about fifty back then—which is my age now. His mother was maybe seventy-five, with eight more years to go until she tried to rescue a bat she found clinging upside down to her living room draperies.

Mr. Barry was a self-educated inventor and super-salesman. He had entered the armaments business more or less by accident. The timer on an automatic washing machine which he had been manufacturing in the old Keedsler Automobile Works turned out to have military applications. It was ideal for timing the release of bombs from airplanes—so as to create a desired pattern of explosions on the ground. When the war was over, orders for much more sophisticated weapons systems started coming in, and Mr. Barry brought in more and more brilliant scientists and engineers and technicians to keep up with the game.

A lot of them were Japanese. My father played host to the first Italians to settle in Midland City. Mr. Barry brought in the first Japanese.

I'll never forget the first Japanese to come into Schramm's Drugstore when I was on all-night duty there. I have mentioned that the store was a lighthouse for lunatics—and that Japanese was a lunatic of a sort, almost literally a lunatic, since the word "lunatic" has to do with craziness and the moon. This Japanese didn't want to buy anything. He wanted me to come outside and see something wonderful in the moonlight.

Guess what it was. It was the conical slate roof of my childhood home, only a few blocks away. The peak of the cone, where the cupola used to be, was capped with very light gray tar roofing, with bits of sand stuck to it. In the light of a full moon, it was glittering white—like snow.

The Japanese smiled and pointed up at the roof. He had no idea that the building meant anything to me. Here was the thought he wanted to share with me, the only other person awake at the time: "Fujiyama," he said, "—the sacred volcano of Japan."

• • •

Mr. Barry, like a lot of self-educated people, was full of obscure facts which he had found for himself, and which nobody else seemed to know. He asked me, for instance, if I knew Sir Galahad had been a Jew.

I said politely that I hadn't. It was his airplane. I expected to be annoyed by an anti-Semitic joke of some kind. I was mistaken.

"Not even the Jews know Sir Galahad was a Jew," he went on. "Jesus, yes—Galahad no. Every Jew I meet, I ask him, 'How come you people don't boast more about Sir Galahad?' And I even tell them where they can check it out, if they want to. 'Start with the Holy Grail,' I say."

According to Fred T. Barry, a Jew named Joseph of Arimathea took Christ's goblet when the Last Supper was over. He believed Christ to be divine.

Joseph brought the goblet to the Crucifixion, and some of Christ's blood fell into it. Joseph was arrested for his Christian sympathies. He was thrown into prison without food or water, but he survived for several years. He had the goblet with him, and every day it filled up with food and drink.

So the Romans let him go. They couldn't have known about the goblet, or they surely would have taken it from him. And Joseph went to England to spread the word about Christ. The goblet fed him on the way. And this wandering Jew founded the first Christian church in England—at Glastonbury. He stuck his staff into the ground

173

there, and it became a tree which bloomed every Christmas Eve.

Imagine that.

Joseph had children, who inherited the goblet, which came to be known as the "Holy Grail."

But sometime during the next five hundred years, the Holy Grail was lost. King Arthur and his knights would become obsessed with finding it again—the most sacred relic in England. Knight after knight failed. Supernatural messages indicated that their hearts weren't pure enough for them to find the Grail.

But then Sir Galahad presented himself at Camelot, and it was evident to everyone that his heart was perfectly pure. And he did find the Grail. He was not only spiritually entitled to it. He was legally entitled to it as well, since he was the last living descendant of that wandering Jew, Joseph of Arimathea.

• • •

Mr. Barry told me what the "stock" part of a "laughingstock" was. It was a tree stump used as a target by archers. I had told him that I guessed I was the laughingstock of New York.

Fred's mother said to me, speaking of herself, "Shake hands with the laughingstock of Midland City, and the laughingstock of Venice, Italy, and the laughingstock of Madrid, Spain, and the laughingstock of Vancouver, British Columbia, and the laughingstock of Cairo, Egypt, and of just about every important city you can name."

• • •

Felix got to talking to the pilot, Tiger Adams, about Celia Hildreth, who had become Celia Hoover. Tiger, who had been a year ahead of Felix in high school, had taken her out once, which was par for the course. He guessed that she was lucky to have married an automobile dealer who didn't care what was under her hood.

"A cream puff," he said. At that time, this was a common description for an automobile which was flashy and loaded with accessories—and never mind whether it ran or not.

He had one interesting piece of information, which I had also heard: that the place to see Celia was at the YMCA at night, where she was enrolled in several self-improvement programs—calligraphy and modern dance and business law, and things like that. This had been going on for a couple of years or more.

Felix, hunching forward, asked Adams how Dwayne Hoover took it, having his wife go off night after night. And Adams replied that Dwayne had probably given up interesting her in sex. It was a futile undertaking. Dwayne was consoling himself, no doubt, in somebody else's arms.

"And that's probably a chore for him," Adams went on, "like having his teeth cleaned." He laughed. "It's something everybody should do at least twice a year," he said.

"Some sexy town," said Felix.

"Some towns had better pay attention to business,"

said Adams. "It would be a terrible thing for the country if
they were all like Hollywood and New York."

• • •

And after we set down on the one runway that was
open at Cincinnati, it was evident to me that the runway
had been cleared at great expense and just for us. That was
how important Fred T. Barry was. It turned out that he
was on an emergency mission, although he and his mother
had said nothing about that to us. The Air Force was
deeply concerned about sensitive work that Barrytron was
doing for them. They had a helicopter waiting to take him
straight to Midland City, so that he could evaluate and
remedy any damage the blizzard might have done to the
plant.

In order that we might come along with him, Mr.
Barry said that Felix and I were two of his top executives.
So up we went again, this time in a clattering contraption
invented by Leonardo da Vinci. Leonardo had obviously
modeled it on some mythological creature—half eagle, half
cow.

That was Fred T. Barry's image: "Half eagle, half
cow."

He made me a present of another image, too, as the
shadow of our heavier-than-air machine skittered over the
unbroken snowfield where Route 53, the highway from
Cincinnati to Midland City, used to be.

I was in a permanent cringe in my seat, going over in
my mind all the terrible things about the blizzard which I

had heard and read in New York. Thousands were obviously dying or dead below us. It would take a long time to find all the bodies, and there would be so much rebuilding to do. Midland City and Shepherdstown, when the snow melted, would look like French towns on the front in the First World War.

But Fred T. Barry, as cheerful as ever, said to me, "It's nothing but a big pillow fight."

"Sir—?" I said.

"Human beings always treat blizzards as though they were the end of the world," he said. "They're like birds when the sun goes down. Birds think the sun is never going to come up again. Sometime, just listen to the birds when the sun goes down."

"Sir—?" I said.

"This will all melt in a few days or a few weeks," he said, "and it will turn out that everybody is all right, and nothing much got hurt. You'll hear on the news that so-and-so many people were killed by the blizzard, but they would have died anyway. Somebody dies of cancer he's had for eleven years, and the radio says the blizzard got him."

So I relaxed some. I sat up straighter.

"Blizzard is nothing but a great big pillow fight," he said.

His mother laughed. Mother and son were so unvain and unafraid. They had such nice times.

• • •

But Fred T. Barry must have been temporarily re-gretful that he'd said that—when we got a good look from the air at the carriage house. We had circled over the city, so we approached the conical roof from the north. Wind had piled snow halfway up the big north window. The drift hid the back door, the kitchen door, entirely. Seeing it from a distance, I imagined that the drift would actually make the place cozier, would shield it from the wind.

But we were horrified when we saw the south side. The great doors, which had last been thrown open for Celia Hildreth in 1943, were agape again. The back door had blown open, we would find out later, and the gale it admitted had flung open the great doors from the inside. The enormous open doorway appeared to have tried to vomit the snow which had piled up inside. How deep was the snow inside? Six feet or more.

21

F_{RED} T. B_{ARRY} and his mother were left off by the helicopter on a rooftop at Barrytron. Mr. Barry maintained the hoax that Felix and I were his employees, and he instructed the pilot sternly that he was to take us wherever we wanted to go, and to stand by until we were through with him. We had all been such great pals, and gone through so much together, and the mood was that we should really see a lot more of each other, and that most people in Midland City weren't as amusing and worldly as we were, and so on.

But I would not see or hear from Mr. Barry for ten more years, and I would never lay eyes on his mother again. Out of sight, out of mind. That's how it was with the Barrys.

So Felix and I used that Air Force helicopter like a taxicab. We went back to the carriage house. There were no footprints there. We had jackets and hats and gloves, but no boots. We were wearing ordinary street shoes, and these filled with snow as we wallowed and tumbled and writhed our way inside. Maybe Mother and Father were under all that snow. If so, they were dead.

We got to the staircase, whose bottom half was buried. Knowing our parents, we supposed that they had gone to bed when the blizzard hit. They wouldn't have got out of bed, we surmised, even after all hell cut loose downstairs. So Felix and I entered their bedroom. The bed was empty. Not only that, but it was stripped of its blankets and sheets. So, maybe Mother and Father had wrapped themselves in bedding, and gone downstairs after all.

I went up one more flight to what used to be the gun room, while Felix checked the other rooms on the loft.

We were expecting to find bodies as hard and stiff as andirons. It was so cold inside. These words popped into my head: "Dead storage."

I heard Felix call from the balcony: "Anybody home?" And then, as I came down from the gun room, he looked up at me, and he said, haggardly, "Nice to be home again."

. . .

We found Mother and Father at the County Hospital. Father was dying of double pneumonia, coupled with kidney failure. Mother had frostbitten fingers and feet. Father was very sick before the blizzard ever hit, and had been about to go to the hospital anyway.

Before the streets became completely impassable, Mother had walked out into the storm in a bathrobe and bedroom slippers and a nightgown, with the Hungarian Life Guard tunic over her shoulders and the sable busby on her head. She was out there long enough to suffer frostbite, but she managed to flag down a snowplow. And the snowplow took her and Father, all bundled up in bedclothes, to the hospital, which had its own diesel-powered electric plant.

When Felix and I came into the lobby of the hospital, not knowing if our parents were there or not, we were appalled by the mess. Hundreds of healthy people had sought shelter there, although nobody was supposed to go there unless seriously ill. The sanitary facilities were swamped, and the refugees had begun to infest the entire hospital, in search of food and water and places to lie down.

These were my people. They had become pioneers again. They were starting a new settlement.

They were ten deep at the information counter, which Felix and I were trying to approach, too. You would have thought it was a bar on the Klondike. So I told Felix that I would keep trying to get up to the counter, while he went looking for familiar faces which might have news of our parents.

I had a feeling, while I inched forward in the crowd, that invisible insects were buzzing around my head. The hospital lobby was surely hot and humid enough for real insects, but the ones that nagged and niggled around me were a condition of my spirit. There had been no such swarms in New York City, but here they were again in my own hometown. They were little bits of information I had about this person or that person, or which this or that person had about me.

I was a Midland City celebrity, of course, so every so often I heard or thought I heard these words: "Deadeye Dick."

I gave no sign that I heard them. What would have been the point of my looking this or that person in the eye, accusing him or her of having called me "Deadeye Dick"? I deserved the name.

When I got to within a rank of the information counter, I learned that the other people were there principally to gain some measure of respect. No truly urgent questions were being put to the three frazzled women behind the counter.

Typical questions:

"What's the latest news, miss?"

"If we want blankets, where do we go?"

"Do you know that they're out of toilet paper in the ladies' room?"

"How sick do you have to be to get a room?"

"Could I have some dimes for when the telephones start working again?"

"Is that clock right?"

"Can we use just one burner in the kitchen for about fifteen minutes?"

"Dr. Mitchell is my doctor. I'm not sick, but would you please tell him I'm here anyway?"

"Is there a list of everybody who's here? Do you want my name?"

"Is there some office where they'll cash a personal check for me?"

"Can I help some way?"

"My mother's got this pain in her left leg that won't go away. What should I do?"

"What is the Power and Light Company doing?"

"Should I tell somebody that I've got a legful of shrapnel from the First World War?"

I came to admire the three women behind the counter. They were patient and polite, for the most part. One of them blew up ever so briefly at the man with the legful of shrapnel. Her initial reply had somehow left him unsatisfied, and he told her that she had no business in the medical profession, if she wouldn't listen to what people were trying to tell her about themselves. I had a vague idea who he was, and I had my doubts about his ever having been in any war. I was pretty sure he was one of the Gatch brothers, who used to work for the Maritimo Brothers Construction Company, until they were caught stealing tools and building materials.

If he was who I was pretty sure he was, he had a daughter who was two years ahead of me in school, Mary or Martha or Marie, maybe, who was a shoplifter. She was always trying to turn people into friends by making them presents of things she stole.

And the woman behind the counter told him bitterly that she was just an ordinary housewife, who had volunteered to help at the hospital, and that she hadn't been to sleep for twenty-four hours. It was late afternoon by then.

I realized that I knew who she was, too—not approximately, but exactly. Twenty-four hours of sleeplessness had made her, in my eyes, anyway, an idealized representative of compassionate, long-suffering women of all ages everywhere. She denied that she was a nurse, but she was a nurse anyway, without vanity or guile.

I have a tendency, anyway, to swoon secretly in the presence of nurturing women, since my own mother was such a cold and aggressively helpless old bat.

Who was this profoundly beautiful and unselfish woman behind the counter? What a surprise! This was Celia Hoover, née Hildreth, the wife of the Pontiac dealer—once believed to be the dumbest girl in high school. I wanted Felix to get a look at her, but I could not spot him anywhere. The last time he had seen her, she had been cutting through a vacant lot in the nighttime, way back in 1943.

• • •

She was a robot in back of the counter. Her memory was blasted by weariness. I asked her if Mr. and Mrs. Otto Waltz were in the hospital, and she looked in a card file. She told me mechanically that Otto Waltz was in intensive care, in critical condition, and could not have visitors, and that Emma Wetzel Waltz was not in serious condition, and had been given a bed in a makeshift ward which had been set up in the basement.

So there was a member of our distinguished family down in a basement again.

I had never been in the basement of the hospital before. But I had known this much about it even when I was a little boy: That was where they had the city morgue.

That had been the first stop for Eloise Metzger, after I shot her between the eyes.

• • •

I found Felix standing in a corner of the lobby, agog at the crowd. He hadn't done anything to try and find Mother and Father. He was useless. "Help me, Rudy," he said, "—I'm seventeen years old again." It was true.

"Somebody just called me the 'Velvet Fog,' " he marveled. This was the sobriquet of a famous singer of popular music named Mel Tormé. Felix had also been nicknamed that in high school.

"Whoever called me that," he said, "said it sneeringly, as though I should be ashamed of myself. It was a real fat guy, with cold blue eyes. A grown man in a business suit. Nobody's spoken to me like that since the Army took me away from here."

It was easy for me to guess who he was talking about. It had to be Jerry Mitchell, who had been Felix's worst enemy in high school. "Jerry Mitchell," I said.

"That was Jerry?" said Felix. "He's so heavy. He's lost so much hair!"

"Not only that," I said, "but he's a doctor now."

"I pity his patients," said Felix. "He used to torture

cats and dogs, and say he was performing scientific experiments."

And there was prophecy in that. Dr. Mitchell was building a big practice on the principle that nobody in modern times should ever be the least uncomfortable or dissatisfied, since there were now pills for everything. And he would buy himself a great big house out in Fairchild Heights, right next door to Dwayne and Celia Hoover, and he would encourage Celia and his own wife, and God only knows who all else, to destroy their minds and spirits with amphetamine.

About that insect swarm around my head, all those bits of information I had on this person and that one: Dr. Jerome Mitchell was married to the former Barbara Squires, the younger sister of Anthony Squires. Anthony Squires was the policeman who had given me the nickname Deadeye Dick.

• • •

Father's deathbed scene went like this: Mother and Felix and I were there, right by his bed. Gino and Marco Maritimo, faithful to the end, had driven to the hospital atop their own bulldozer. It would later turn out that these two endearing old poops had done hundreds of thousands of dollars' worth of damage on the way, tearing up hidden automobiles and fences and fire hydrants and mailboxes, and so on. They had to stay out in the corridor, since they weren't blood relatives.

Father was under an oxygen tent. He was all shot up
with antibiotics, but his body couldn't fight off the pneumonia. Too much else was wrong. The hospital had shaved
off his thick, youthful hair and mustache, so that an accidental spark couldn't make them burn like gunpowder in
the presence of all that oxygen. He seemed to be asleep,
but having nightmares, fighting with his eyes closed, when
Felix and I came in.

Mother had already been there for hours. Her
frostbitten hands and feet were enclosed in plastic bags
filled with a yellow salve, so that she couldn't touch any of
us. This turned out to be an experimental treatment for
frostbite, invented right there in Midland City that very
morning, by a Doctor Miles Pendleton. We assumed that
all frostbite victims had their damaged parts encased in
plastic and salve. Mother, in fact, was probably the only
person in history to be treated that way.

She was a human guinea pig, and we didn't even
know it.

No harm done, luckily.

• • •

Father's peephole closed forever at sunset on the day
after the opening and closing of my play. He was sixty-
eight. The only word Felix and I heard from him was his
very last one, which was this: "Mama." It was Mother who
told us about his earlier deathbed assertions—that he had at
least been good with children, that he had always tried to

behave honorably, and that he hoped he had at least brought some appreciation of beauty to Midland City, even if he himself hadn't been an artist.

• • •

He mentioned guns, according to Mother, but he didn't editorialize about them. All he said was, "Guns."

The wrecked guns, including the fatal Springfield, had been donated to a scrap drive during the war—along with the weather vane. They might have killed a lot more people when they were melted up and made into shells or bombs or hand grenades or whatever.

Waste not, want not.

• • •

As far as I know, he had only one big secret which he might have told on his deathbed: Who killed August Gunther, and what became of Gunther's head. But he didn't tell it. Who would have cared? Would there have been any social benefit in prosecuting old Francis X. Morissey, who had become chief of police and was about to retire, for accidentally blowing Gunther's head off with a ten-gauge shotgun forty-four years ago?

Let sleeping dogs lie.

• • •

When Felix and I got to Father, he was a baby again. He thought his mother was somewhere around. He died believing that he had once owned one of the ten greatest paintings in the world. This wasn't "The Minorite Church of Vienna" by Adolf Hitler. Father had nothing to say about Hitler as he died. He had learned his lesson about Hitler. One of the ten greatest paintings in the world, as far as he was concerned, was "Crucifixion in Rome," by John Rettig, which he had bought for a song in Holland, during his student days. It now hangs in the Cincinnati Art Museum.

"Crucifixion in Rome," in fact, was one of the few successes in the art marketplace, or in any sort of marketplace, which Father experienced in his threescore years and eight. When he and Mother had to put up all their treasures for sale, in order to pay off the Metzgers, they had imagined that their paintings alone were worth hundreds of thousands of dollars. They advertised in an art magazine, I remember, that an important art collection was to be liquidated, and that serious collectors and museum curators could see it by appointment in our house.

About five people did come all the way to Midland City for a look, I remember, and found the collection ludicrous. One man, I remember, wanted a hundred pictures for a motel he was furnishing in Biloxi, Mississippi. The rest really seemed to know and care about art.

But the only painting anybody wanted was "Crucifixion in Rome." The Cincinnati Art Museum bought it for not much money, and the museum wanted it not because its greatness was so evident, I'm sure, but because it had been painted by a native of Cincinnati. It was a tiny thing, about the size of a shirt cardboard—about the size of Father's work in progress, the nude in his Vienna studio.

John Rettig, in fact, died in the year I was born, which was 1932. Unlike me, he got out of his hometown and stayed out. He took off for the Near East and then Europe, and he finally settled in Volendam, Holland. That became his home, and that was where Father discovered him before the First World War.

Volendam was John Rettig's Katmandu. When Father met him, this man from Cincinnati was wearing wooden shoes.

• • •

"Crucifixion in Rome" is signed "John Rettig," and it is dated 1888. So it was painted four years before Father was born. Father must have bought it in 1913 or so. Felix thinks there is a possibility that Hitler was with Father on that skylarking trip to Holland. Maybe so.

"Crucifixion in Rome" is indeed set in Rome, which I have never seen. I know enough, though, to recognize that it is chock-a-block with architectural anachronisms. The Colosseum, for example, is in perfect repair, but there is also the spire of a Christian church, and some architectural details and monuments which appear to be more recent, even, than the Renaissance, maybe even nineteenth century. There are sixty-eight tiny but distinct human figures taking part in some sort of celebration amid all this architecture and sculpture. Felix and I counted them one time, when we were young. Hundreds more are implied by impressionistic smears and dots. Banners fly. Walls are festooned with ropes of leaves. What fun.

Only if you look closely at the painting will you realize that two of the sixty-eight figures are not having such a good time. They are in the lower left-hand corner, and are harmonious with the rest of the composition, but they have in fact just been hung from crosses.

The picture is a comment, I suppose, but certainly a bland one, on man's festive inhumanity to men—even into what to John Rettig were modern times.

It has the same general theme, I guess, of Picasso's "Guernica," which I have seen. I went to see "Guernica" at the Museum of Modern Art in New York City, during a lull in the rehearsals of *Katmandu*.

Some picture!

22

I WENT FOR A WALK through hospital corridors all alone after Father died. A few people may or may not have murmured "Deadeye Dick" behind my back. It was a busy place.

I came upon strange beauty unexpectedly in a fourth-floor cul-de-sac. It was in a dazzlingly sunny patients' lounge. The unexpected beauty was in the form of Celia Hoover, née Hildreth, again. She had fallen asleep on a couch, and her eleven-year-old son was watching over her. She had evidently brought him with her to the hospital, rather than leave him alone at home in the blizzard.

He was seated stiffly on the edge of the couch. Even in sleep, she was keeping him captive. She was holding his hand. I had the feeling that, if he had tried to get up, she would have awakened enough to make him sit back down again.

That seemed all right with him.

• • •

Yes—well—and ten years later, in 1970, that same boy would be a notorious homosexual, living away from home in the old Fairchild Hotel. His father, Dwayne Hoover, had disowned him. His mother had become a recluse. He eked out a living as a piano player at night in the Tally-ho Room of the new Holiday Inn.

I was again what I had been before the fiasco of my play in New York, the all-night man at Schramm's Drugstore. Father was buried in Calvary Cemetery, not all that far from Eloise Metzger. We buried him in a painter's smock, and with his left thumb hooked through a palette. Why not?

The city had taken the old carriage house for fifteen years of back taxes. The first floor now sheltered the carcasses of trucks and buses which were being cannibalized for parts. The upper floors were dead storage for documents relating to transactions by the city before the First World War.

Mother and I inhabited a little two-bedroom shitbox out in the Maritimo Brothers development known as "Avondale." Mother and I moved into it about three months after Father died. It was virtually a gift from Gino and Marco Maritimo. We didn't even have a down payment. Mother and I were both dead broke, and Felix hadn't started to make really big money yet, and he was about to pay alimony to two ex-wives instead of one. Old Gino and Marco told us to move in anyway, and not to worry. The price they were asking, it turned out, was so far below the actual value of the house that we had no trouble getting a mortgage. It had been a model house, too, which meant it was already landscaped, and there were Venetian blinds already on all the windows, and a flagstone walk running up to the front door, and a post lantern out front, and all sorts of expensive options which most Avondale buyers passed up, like a full basement and genuine tile in the bathroom, and a cedar closet in Mother's bedroom, and a dishwasher and a garbage disposal unit and a wall oven and a built-in breakfast nook in the kitchen, and a fireplace with an ornate mantelpiece in the living room, and an outdoor barbecue, and an eight-foot cedar fence around the backyard, and on and on.

• • •

So, in 1970, at the age of thirty-eight, I was still cooking for my mother, and making her bed every day, and doing her laundry, and so on. My brother, forty-four then, was president of the National Broadcasting Company, and living in a penthouse overlooking Central Park, and one of the ten best-dressed men in the country, supposedly, and breaking up with his fourth wife. According to a gossip column Mother and I read, he and his fourth wife had divided the penthouse in half with a line of chairs. Neither one was supposed to go in the other one's territory.

Felix was also due to be fired any day, according to the same column, because the ratings of NBC prime time television shows were falling so far behind those of the other networks.

Felix denied this.

· · ·

Yes—and Fred T. Barry had lost his mother, and the Maritimo Brothers Construction Company was building the Mildred Barry Memorial Center for the Arts on stilts in the middle of Sugar Creek. I hadn't seen Mr. Barry for ten years.

But Tiger Adams, his pilot, came into Schramm's Drugstore one morning, at about two A.M. I asked him how Mr. Barry was, and he said that he had almost no interest in anything anymore, except for the arts center.

"He says he wants to give southwestern Ohio its own Taj Mahal," he told me. "He's sick with loneliness, of course. If it weren't for the arts center, I think maybe he would have killed himself."

So I looked up the Taj Mahal at the downtown public library the next afternoon. The library was about to be torn down, since the neighborhood had deteriorated so much. Nice people didn't like to go there anymore in the winter, since there were always so many bums inside, just keeping warm.

I had of course heard of the Taj Mahal before. Who hasn't? And it had figured in my play. Old John Fortune saw the Taj Mahal before he died. That was the last place he sent a postcard from. But I had never known why and when and how it had been built, exactly.

It turned out that it was completed in 1643, three hundred and one years before I shot Eloise Metzger. It took twenty thousand workmen twenty-two years to build it.

It was a memorial to something Fred T. Barry never had, and which I have never had, which is a wife. Her name was Arjumand Banu Begum. She died in childbirth. Her husband, who ordered the Taj Mahal to be built at any cost, was the Mogul emperor Shah Jahan.

• • •

Tiger Adams gave me news of somebody else I hadn't seen for quite a while. He said that, two nights before, he had been coming in for a night landing at Will Fairchild Memorial Airport, and he had had to pull up at the last second because there was somebody out on the runway.

Whoever it was fell down in a heap right in the middle of the runway, and then just stayed there. There were only two people inside the airport at that hour—one in the tower, and the other waxing floors down below. So the floor waxer, who was one of the Gatch brothers, drove out on the runway in his own car.

He had to half-drag the mystery person into his car. It turned out to be Celia Hoover. She was barefoot, and wearing her husband's trenchcoat over a nightgown, and about five miles from home. She had evidently gone for a long walk, even though she was barefoot—and she had got on the runway in the dark, thinking it was a road. And then the landing lights had come on all of a sudden, and the Barrytron Learjet had put a part in her hair.

Nobody notified the police or anybody. Gatch just took her home.

Gatch later told Tiger then there hadn't been anybody at her house to wonder where she had been, to be relieved that she was all right, and so on. She just went inside all alone, and presumably went to bed all alone. After she went inside, one light upstairs went on for about three minutes, and then went off again. It looked like a bathroom light.

According to Tiger, Gatch said this to the blacked-out house: "Sleep tight, honeybunch."

• • •

That isn't quite right. There had been a dog to welcome her home, but she hadn't paid any attention to the dog. She had put no value, as far as Gatch could see, on the dog's delight. She didn't pet it or thank it, or anything—or tell it to come on upstairs with her.

The dog was Dwayne Hoover's Labrador retriever, Sparky, but Dwayne was hardly ever home anymore. Sparky would have been glad to see just about anybody. Sparky was glad to see Gatch.

• • •

So, while I try not to become too concerned about anybody, while my feeling ever since I shot Eloise

Metzger has been that I don't really belong on this particular planet, I had loved Celia at least a little bit. She had been in my play, after all, and had taken the play very seriously—which made her a sort of child or sister of mine.

To have been a perfectly uninvolved person, a perfect neuter, I should never have written a play.

To have been a perfect neuter, I shouldn't have bought a new Mercedes, either. That's correct: Ten years after Father died, I had saved so much money, working night after night, and living so modestly out in Avondale, that I bought a white, four-door Mercedes 280, and still had plenty of money left over.

It felt like a very funny accident. There Deadeye Dick was all of a sudden, driving this big white dreamboat around town, evidently talking to himself a mile a minute. What I was really doing, of course, was chasing the blues with scat singing. "Feedily watt a boo boo," I'd sing in my Mercedes, and "Rang-a-dang wee," and so on. "Foodily at! Foodily at!"

• • •

The most troubling news Tiger Adams had about Celia was this: During the seven years since she had been in my play, she had become as ugly as the Wicked Witch of the West in *The Wizard of Oz*.

Those were Tiger's exact words to me: "My God, Rudy, you wouldn't believe it—that poor woman has be-

KURT VONNEGUT

come as ugly as the Wicked Witch of the West in *The Wizard of Oz*."

. . .

A week later, she paid me a call at the drugstore—at about midnight, the witching hour.

23

I HAD JUST COME to work. I was standing at the back door, gazing at my new Mercedes, and listening to the seeming muted roar of waves breaking on a beach not far away. The seeming surf was in fact the sound of gigantic trucks with eighteen wheels, moving at high speed on the Interstate. The night was balmy. All I needed was a ukulele. I was so content.

My back was to the stock room, with its cures for every ailment known to man. A little bell dinged in the stock room, telling me that someone had just entered the front of the store. It could be a killer, of course. There was always a chance that it was a killer, or at least a robber. In the ten years since Father had died, I had been robbed in the store six times.

What a hero I was.

So I went to wait on the customer, or whatever it was. I left the back door unlocked. If it was a robber, I would try to get out the back door and hide among the weeds and garbage cans. He or she would have to help himself or herself. I would not be there to obey his or her orders to cooperate.

The customer, or whatever it was, was inspecting dark glasses on a carousel. Who needed dark glasses at midnight?

It was small for a human being. But it was certainly big enough to carry a sawed-off shotgun under its voluminous trenchcoat, the hem of which scarcely cleared the floor.

"Can I help you?" I said cheerily. Perhaps it had a headache or hemorrhoids.

It faced me, and it showed me the raddled, snaggle-toothed ruins of the face of Celia Hoover, once the most beautiful girl in town.

Again—my memory writes a playlet.

The curtain rises on the interior of a seedy drugstore in the poorest part of a small Middle-Western city, shortly after midnight. RUDY WALTZ, *a fat, neutered pharmacist, is shocked to recognize a demented speed freak, a hag, as* CELIA HOOVER, *once the most beautiful girl in town.*

RUDY: Mrs. Hoover!
CELIA: My hero!
RUDY: Not me.
CELIA: Yes! Yes! You! My hero of theatrical literature!
RUDY (*pained*): Oh, please—
CELIA: That play of yours—it changed my life.
RUDY: You were certainly good in it.

CELIA: All those wonderful words that came out of me—
those were your words. I could never have thought up
words that beautiful to say in a million years. I almost
lived and died without ever saying anything worth
listening to.

RUDY: You made my words sound a lot better than they
really were.

CELIA: I was on that stage, and there were all these people
out there, all bug-eyed, hearing all those wonderful
words coming out of dumb old Celia Hoover. They
couldn't believe it.

RUDY: It was a magic time in my life, too.

CELIA (imitating the audience): "Author! Author!"

RUDY: We were the toast of the town at curtain call. Now,
then—what can I get you here?

CELIA: A new play.

RUDY: I've written my first and last play, Celia.

CELIA: Wrong! I have come to inspire you—with this new
face of mine. Look at my new face! Make up the
words that should come out of a face like this. Write
a crazy-old-lady play!

RUDY (looking out at the street): Where did you park your
car?

CELIA: I always wanted a face like this. I wish I could have
been born with a face like this. It would have saved a
lot of trouble. Everybody could have said, "Just leave
that crazy old lady alone."

RUDY: Is your husband home?

CELIA: You're my husband. That's what I came to tell you.

RUDY: Celia—you are not well. What's your doctor's name?

CELIA: You are my doctor. You are the only person in this town who ever made me glad to be alive—with the medicine of your magic words! Give me more words!

RUDY: You've lost your shoes.

CELIA: I threw my shoes away! In your honor! I threw all my shoes away. They're all in the garbage can.

RUDY: How did you get here?

CELIA: I walked here—and I'll walk home again.

RUDY: There's broken glass everywhere in this neighborhood.

CELIA: I would gladly walk over glowing coals for you. I love you. I need you so.

(RUDY *considers this declaration, comes to a cynical conclusion, which makes him tired.*)

RUDY *(emptily):* Pills.

CELIA: What a team we'd make—the crazy old lady and Deadeye Dick.

RUDY: You want pills from me—without a prescription.

CELIA: I love you.

RUDY: Sure. But it's pills, not love, that make people walk over broken glass at midnight. What'll it be, Celia—amphetamine?

CELIA: As a matter of fact—

RUDY: As a matter of fact—?

CELIA *(as though it were a perfectly routine order, certain to be filled):* Pennwalt Biphetamine, please.

RUDY: "Black beauties."

CELIA: I've never heard them called that.

RUDY: You know how black and glistening they are.

CELIA: You heard what I call them.

RUDY: You can't get them here.

CELIA (indignantly): They've been prescribed for me for years!

RUDY: I'll bet they have! But you've never been here before—with or without a prescription.

CELIA: I came here to ask you to write another play.

RUDY: You came here because you've been shut off every-place else. And I wouldn't give you any more of that poison, if you had a prescription signed by God Almighty. Now you're going to tell me you don't love me after all.

CELIA: I can't believe you're so mean.

RUDY: And who was it who was so nice to you for so long? Dr. Mitchell, I'll bet—hand in hand with the Fairchild Heights Pharmacy. Too late, they got scared to death of what they'd done to you.

CELIA: What makes you so afraid of love?

(Telephone behind prescription counter rings. RUDY goes to answer.)

RUDY: Excuse me. *(Into telephone)* Schramm's *(He listens to a brief question blankly)* So they say. *(He hangs up)* Somebody wanted to know if I was Deadeye Dick. Now, then, Mrs. Hoover—my understanding of the effects of long-term use of amphetamine leads me to expect that you will very soon become abusive. I can take that if I have to, but I'd rather get you home some way.

CELIA: You think you know so much.

RUDY: Is there someplace I can reach your husband? Is he home?

CELIA: Detroit.

RUDY: Your son's just a few blocks away.

CELIA: I hate his guts, and he hates mine.

RUDY: We seem to be living the crazy-old-lady play. I'll call Dr. Mitchell.

CELIA: He's not my doctor anymore. Dwayne beat him up last week—for giving me all those pills so long.

RUDY: Good for Dwayne.

CELIA: Isn't that nice? And as soon as Dwayne gets back from Detroit, he's going to put me in the crazy house.

RUDY: You do need help. You need a lot of help.

CELIA: Then put your arms around me! (RUDY *freezes*) And no Pennwalt Biphetamine, either. No anything here. (*She gravely sweeps a display of cosmetics from a counter to the floor*)

RUDY: Please don't do any more of that.

CELIA: Oh—I'll pay for all damages, any damages I decide to do. Money is not a problem. (*She brings forth a handful of gold coins from her trench-coat pocket*) See?

RUDY: Gold pieces!

CELIA: Sure! I don't fool around. My husband's a coin collector, you know.

RUDY: There's got to be several thousand dollars there.

CELIA: Yours, all yours, honeybunch. *(She scatters the coins at his feet)* Now give me a hug, or give me some Pennwalt Biphetamine.

(RUDY goes to the telephone, dials.)

RUDY *(singing softly to himself, waiting for an answer on the phone)*: Skeedee-wah, skeedee-woo. *(Etc.)*

CELIA: Who are you calling?

RUDY: The police.

CELIA: You big tub of lard! *(She topples a carousel of dark glasses.)* You fat Nazi bastard!

RUDY *(into telephone)*: This is Rudy Waltz—over at Schramm's. Who's this? Oh—Bob! I didn't recognize your voice. I need a little help here.

CELIA: You need a lot of help here! *(She sets about wrecking everything she can get her hands on)* Killer! Mama's boy!

RUDY *(into telephone)*: Not a criminal matter. It's a mental case.

(Curtain.)

. . .

But she got out of there before the police could come. When they arrived, they could see all the damage she had done, but she herself was roaming shoeless out in the night again. That is the second story I have told about Celia which ends with her fleeing barefoot.

History repeats itself.

The police went looking for her—to protect her. She could get robbed or raped. She could be attacked by dogs. She could be hit by a car.

Meanwhile, I set about cleaning up the mess she had made. The store wasn't mine, so I was in no position to forgive and forget. Celia's husband was going to have to find out what she had done, and then he would be asked to cough up a thousand dollars or more. Celia had gone after the most expensive perfumes. Celia had gone after the watches, too, but they were still okay. It is virtually impossible to harm a Timex watch. For some reason, the less you pay for a watch, the surer you can be that it will never stop.

My conscience was active as I worked. Should I have hugged her or given her amphetamine? My feeling was that chemicals had wrecked her brains, and that she wasn't Celia Hoover anymore. She was a monster. If I did write a play for her new face, I thought, she wouldn't be able to learn her lines. Somebody else would have to play her—in a fright wig, and with several teeth blacked out.

What wonderful things could a writer put into the mouth of a crazy old lady like her anyway? My mind got this far with the problem, anyway: She could certainly shake up an audience if she let it think she was about a hundred years old for a while, and then told her true age. Celia was only forty-four when she took the drugstore apart.

I tinkered, too, with the idea of having the voice of God coming from the back of the theater. Whoever played God would have to have a voice like my brother's.

The actress playing Celia could ask why God had ever put her on earth.

And then the voice from the back of the theater could rumble: "To reproduce. Nothing else really interests Me. All the rest is frippery."

· · ·

She had reproduced, of course, which was certainly more than I had done. And I got it into my head to stop cleaning up for a minute and call up her son, Bunny. He would probably be in his room at the Fairchild Hotel, fresh home from work at the new Holiday Inn.

He was wide awake. Somebody had told me that Bunny was heavily into cocaine. That could merely be a rumor.

I told him who I was, and I said his mother had just been in the store, and that, in my opinion, she really needed help. "I just thought you should know," I said.

Out of the corner of my eye, I saw that a mouse was listening to me. It was going to have to guess what was going on, since it could hear only my half of the conversation.

So this disinherited young homosexual at the other end of the line laughed and laughed. Bunny wouldn't make any specific comments on his mother's poor health. His laughter was a terrible thing to hear. He sure hated her.

But then he settled down some, and he told me that maybe I should spend more time worrying about my own relatives.

"What do you mean by that?" I said. The little ears of the mouse were fine-tuning themselves to my voice, not wishing to miss a syllable.

"Your brother's just been canned by NBC," he said.

I said that that was just gossip.

He said it wasn't gossip anymore. He had just heard it over the radio. "It's official," he said. "They finally caught up with him."

"What is that supposed to mean?" I asked him.

"He's just another big fake from Midland City," he said. "Everybody here is fake."

"That's a nice thing to say about your own home-town," I said.

"Your father was a fake. He couldn't paint good pictures. I'm a fake. I can't really play the piano. You're a fake. You can't write decent plays. It's perfectly all right, as long as we all stay home. That's where your brother made his mistake. He went away from home. They catch fakes out in the real world, you know. They catch 'em all the time."

He laughed some more, and I hung up on him.

But then the phone rang right away, and it was my brother calling from his penthouse in Manhattan. It was absolutely true, he said. It was official: He had been canned. "It's the best thing that ever happened to me," he said.

"If that's the case, I'm glad for you," I said. I was standing there, with broken eyeglasses and gold pieces crunching under my feet. The police had come and gone so quickly that I hadn't had a chance to tell them about the gold.

Gold! Gold! Gold!

"For the first time in my life," said Felix, "I have the opportunity to find out who I really am. From now on, women can see me as a real human being, instead of a high-ranking corporate executive who can make them big shots, too."

I told him that I could see how that might be a relief. His wife at that time was named Charlotte, so I asked him how Charlotte was taking things.

"She is what I am talking about," he said. "She didn't marry Felix Waltz. She married the president of the National Broadcasting Company."

I had never met Charlotte. She had sounded nice enough, the few times I had talked to her on the phone— maybe just a touch insincere. She was trying to treat me like family, I guess. She thought she had to be warm, no matter what I really was. I don't know whether she ever found out I was a murderer.

But now Felix was saying that she was insane.

"That's putting it a little strong, I expect," I said.

It turned out that Charlotte was so mad at him that she had cut all the buttons off his clothes—every coat, every suit, every shirt, every pair of pajamas. Then she had thrown all the buttons down the incinerator.

People can sure get mad at each other. They are liable to do anything.

"What's Mom's reaction?" he said.

"She hasn't heard yet," I said. "I guess it'll be in the paper in the morning."

"Tell her I've never been happier," he said.

"Okay," I said.

"She's going to take it pretty hard, I guess," he said.

"Not as hard as she might have a few months ago," I said. "She's got some exciting problems of her own, for a change."

"She's sick?" he said.

"No, no, no," I said. Of course, she was sick, but I had no way of knowing that. "She's been appointed to the board of directors of the new arts center—"

"You told me," he said. "That was certainly very nice of Fred T. Barry to appoint her."

"Well—now she's fighting him tooth and nail about modern art," I said. "She's raising hell about the first two works of art he's bought, even though he paid for them with his own money."

"That doesn't sound like Mother," said Felix.

"One of them's a statue by Henry Moore—" I said.

"The English sculptor?" said Felix.

"Right. And the other one is a painting by somebody named Rabo Karabekian," I said. "The statue is already in the sculpture garden, and Mother says it's nothing but a figure eight on its side. The picture is supposed to go up just inside the front door, so it's the first thing you see when you come in. It's green. It's about the size of a barn door. It has one vertical orange stripe, and it's called 'The Temptation of Saint Anthony.' Mother wrote a letter to the paper, saying the picture was an insult to the memory of Father, and to the memory of every serious artist who ever lived."

The telephone went dead. I will never know why. It was nothing I did on my end. It could have been caused by something the mouse on my end did. The mouse had gone away. It could have been fooling with the telephone wires in the wall. Or maybe, in the basement of my brother's building in New York City, somebody was putting a tap on his line. Maybe a private detective, working for his wife, wanted to get the goods on him—to be used in a divorce action later on. Anything is possible.

Then the telephone came alive again. Felix was talking about coming home to Midland City to rediscover his roots. He said the exact opposite of what Bunny Hoover had said to me. He said that everybody in New York City was phony, and that it was the people of Midland City who were real. He named a lot of friends from high school. He was going to drink beer with them and go hunting with them.

He mentioned some girls, too. It wasn't quite clear what he could do with them, since they were all married, and had children, or had left town. But he didn't mention Celia Hoover, and I didn't remind him of her—didn't tell him that she had become a crazy old bat, and that she had just taken the drugstore apart.

It's interesting that he didn't mention Celia for this reason: He would later declare, under the influence of drugs a doctor had prescribed for him, that she was the only woman he had ever loved, and that he should have married her.

Celia was dead by then.

24

I WOULD BE GLAD to attempt a detailed analysis of Celia Hoover's character, if I thought her character had much of anything to do with her suicide by Drāno. As a pharmacist, though, I see no reason not to give full credit to amphetamine.

Here is the warning which the law requires as a companion now for each shipment of amphetamine as it leaves the factory:

"Amphetamine has been extensively abused. Tolerance, extreme psychological dependence, and severe social disability have occurred. There are reports of patients who have increased dosages to many times that recommended. Abrupt cessation following prolonged high dosage results in extreme fatigue and mental depression; changes are also noted on the sleep EEG.

"Manifestations of chronic intoxication with amphetamine include severe dermatoses, marked insomnia, irritability, hyperactivity, and personality changes. The most severe manifestation of chronic intoxication is psychosis, often indistinguishable from schizophrenia."

Want some?

• • •

The late twentieth century will go down in history, I'm sure, as an era of pharmaceutical buffoonery. My own brother came home from New York City—bombed on Darvon and Ritalin and methaqualone and Valium, and God only knows what all. He had prescriptions for every bit of it. He said he was home to discover his roots, but, after I heard about all the pills he was taking, I thought he would be lucky to find his own behind with both hands. I thought it was a miracle that he had even found the right exit off the Interstate.

As it was, he had an accident on his way home—in a brand new white Rolls-Royce convertible. The car itself was drug-inspired madness. The day after he was fired and his fourth wife walked out on him, he bought a seventy-thousand-dollar motorcar.

He loaded it up like a truck with his buttonless wardrobe, and took off for Midland City. And when he first got home, his conversation, if you could call it that, was repetitious, obsessed. There were only two things he wanted to do: One was to find his roots, and the other was to find some woman who would sew all his buttons back on. The only buttons he had were on the clothes on his back. He had been particularly vulnerable to an attack on his buttons, too, since his suits and coats were made in London, with buttons instead of zippers on their flies, and with buttons at the wrists which actually buttoned and unbuttoned. He put on one of his buttonless coats for Mother and me, and those floppy cuffs made him look like a pirate in *Peter Pan.*

· · ·

There was a big dent in the left front fender of that brand new Rolls-Royce, and a crease and a sort of chalky blue stripe that ran back from the dent and across the left-hand door. Felix had sideswiped something blue, and he was as curious about what it might have been as we were.

It remains a mystery to the present day, although Felix, I am happy to say, is now drug free, except for alcohol and caffeine, which he uses in moderation. He remembers proposing marriage to a girl he picked up at a tollbooth on the Ohio Turnpike. "She bailed out in downtown Mansfield," he said the other night. He had swung off the turnpike and into Mansfield, to buy her a color television set or a stereo or anything she wanted, as proof of how much he liked her.

"That could have been where I got the dent," he said.

He was able to identify the drug which had made him so brainlessly ardent, too. "Methaqualone," he said.

· · ·

I think now about all the little shitbox houses I have driven by in my life, and that all Americans have driven by in their lives—shitbox houses with very expensive cars in the driveway, and maybe even a yacht on a trailer, too. And suddenly there was Mother's and my little shitbox, with a new Mercedes under the carport, and a new Rolls-Royce convertible on the front lawn. That was where Felix first parked his car when he got home—on the lawn. We were lucky he didn't take down the post lantern, and half the shrubbery, too.

So in he came, saying, "The prodigal son is home! Kill the fatted calf!" and so on. Mother and I had known he was coming, but we hadn't known exactly when. We were all dressed up, and about to go out, and were going to leave the side door unlocked for him.

I was wearing my best suit, which was as tight as the skin of a knackwurst. I had put on a lot of weight recently. It was the fault of my own good cooking. I had been trying out a lot of new recipes, with considerable success. And Mother, who hadn't put on an ounce in fifty years, was wearing the black dress Felix had bought her for Father's funeral.

"Where do you two think you're going?" said Felix.

So Mother told him. "We're going to Celia Hoover's funeral," she said.

That was the first Felix had heard that his date for the senior prom was no longer among the living. The last he had seen of her, she had been running away from him barefoot, and into a vacant lot—at night.

If he was going to catch her now, he would have to go wherever it was that the dead people went.

. . .

That would make a good scene in a movie: Felix in heaven, wearing a tuxedo for the senior prom carrying Celia's golden slippers, and calling out over and over again, "Celia! Celia! Where are you? I have your dancing shoes."

. . .

So nothing would do but that Felix come to the funeral with us. Methaqualone had persuaded him that he and Celia had been high school sweethearts, and that he should have married her. "She was what I was looking for all the time, and I never even realized it," he said.

I think now that Mother and I should have driven him to the County Hospital for detoxification. But we got into his car with him, and told him where the funeral was. The top was down, which was no way to go to a funeral, and Felix himself was a mess. His necktie was askew, and his shirt was filthy, and he had a two-day growth of beard. He had found time to buy a Rolls-Royce, but it hadn't occurred to him that he might have bought some new shirts with buttons, too. He wasn't going to have another shirt with buttons until he could find some woman who would sew all his buttons on.

. . .

Off we went to the First Methodist Church, with Felix at the wheel and Mother in the back seat. As luck would have it, Felix almost closed the peephole of his first wife, Donna, as she was getting out of her Thunderbird in front of her twin sister's house on Arsenal Avenue. It would have been her fault, if she had died, since she didn't look to see what was coming before she disembarked on the driver's side. But it would have made for an ugly case in court, since Felix had already put her through a windshield once, and he was still paying her a lot of alimony, and the business about all the pills he was taking would have come out, and so on. Worst of all, as far as a jury was concerned, I'm sure, would have been the fact that he was a bloated plutocrat in a Rolls-Royce.

Felix didn't even recognize her, and I don't think she recognized him, either. When I told him who it was he had almost hit, he spoke of her most unkindly. He recalled that her scalp was crisscrossed with scars, because of her trip through the windshield. When he used to run his fingers through her hair, he would encounter those scars, and he would get this crazy idea that he was a quarterback. "I would look downfield for an end who was open for a forward pass," he said.

• • •

It was at the church, though, that Felix and his good friend methaqualone became embarrassing. We got there late, so we had to sit toward the back, where those least concerned with the deceased should have been sitting anyway. If we were going to make any disturbance, people would have to swivel around in their pews to see who we were.

The service started quietly enough. I heard only one person crying, and she was way up front, and I think it was Lottie Davis, the Hoovers' black maid. She and Dwayne were the only people there to do a whole lot of crying, since practically nobody else had seen Celia for seven years—since she had starred in *Katmandu*.

Her son wasn't there.

Her doctor wasn't there.

Both her parents were dead, and all her brothers and sisters had drifted off to God-knows-where. One brother, I know, was killed in the Korean War. And somebody swore, I remember, that he had seen her sister Shirley as an extra in the remake of the movie *King Kong*. Maybe so.

There were maybe two hundred mourners there. Most of them were employees and friends and customers and suppliers of Dwayne's. The word was all over town of how in need of support he was, of how vocally ashamed he was to have been such a bad husband that his wife had committed suicide. He had been quoted to me as having made a public announcement in the Tally-ho Room of the new Holiday Inn, the day after Celia killed herself: "I take half the blame, but the other half goes to that son-of-bitching Doctor Jerry Mitchell. Watch out for the pills your doctor tells your wife to take. That's all I've got to say."

• • •

It must have been a startling scene. From five until six thirty or so every weekday night, the Tally-ho Room, the cocktail lounge, was a plenary session of the oligarchy of Midland City. A few powerful people, most notably Fred T. Barry, were involved in planetary games, so that the deliberations at the Tally-ho Room were beneath their notice. But anyone doing big business or hoping to do big business strictly within the county was foolish not to show his face there at least once a week, if only to drink a glass of ginger ale. The Tally-ho Room did a very big trade in ginger ale.

Dwayne owned a piece of the new Holiday Inn, incidentally. His automobile dealership was right next door, on the same continuous sheet of blacktop. And the Tally-ho Room was where his disinherited son, Bunny, played the piano. The story was that Bunny applied for the job there, and the manager of the Inn asked Dwayne how he felt about it, and Dwayne said he had never heard of Bunny, so he did not care if the Inn hired him or not, as long as he could play the piano.

And then Dwayne added, supposedly, that he himself hated piano music, since it interfered with conversation. All he asked was that there be no piano playing until eight o'clock at night. That way, although he did not say so, Dwayne Hoover would never have to lay eyes on his disgraceful son.

• • •

I daydreamed at Celia's funeral. There was no reason to expect that anything truly exciting or consoling would be said. Not even the minister, the Reverend Charles Harrell, believed in heaven or hell. Not even the minister thought that every life had a meaning, and that every death could startle us into learning something important, and so on. The corpse was a mediocrity who had broken down after a while. The mourners were mediocrities who would break down after a while.

The city itself was breaking down. Its center was already dead. Everybody shopped at the outlying malls. Heavy industry had gone bust. People were moving away.

The planet itself was breaking down. It was going to blow itself up sooner or later anyway, if it didn't poison itself first. In a manner of speaking, it was already eating Drāno.

There in the back of the church, I daydreamed a theory of what life was all about. I told myself that Mother and Felix and the Reverend Harrell and Dwayne Hoover and so on were cells in what was supposed to be one great big animal. There was no reason to take us seriously as individuals. Celia in her casket there, all shot through with Drāno and amphetamine, might have been a dead cell sloughed off by a pancreas the size of the Milky Way.

How comical that I, a single cell, should take my life so seriously!

I found myself smiling at a funeral.

I stopped smiling. I glanced around to see if anyone had noticed. One person had. He was at the other end of our pew, and he did not look away when I caught him gazing at me. He went right on gazing, and it was I who faced forward again. I had not recognized him. He was wearing large sunglasses with mirrored lenses. He could have been anyone.

• • •

But then I became the center of attention for the full congregation, for Reverend Harrell had mentioned my name. He was talking about Rudy Waltz. I was Rudy Waltz. To whoever might be watching our insignificant lives under an electron microscope: We cells have names, and, if we know little else, we know our names.

Reverend Harrell told the congregation of the six weeks when he and the late Celia Hoover, née Hildreth, and the playwright Rudy Waltz had known blissful unselfishness which could serve as a good example for the rest of the world. He was talking about the local production of *Katmandu*. He had played the part of John Fortune, the Ohio pilgrim to nowhere, and Celia had played the ghost of his wife. He was a gifted actor. He resembled a lion.

For all I know, Celia may have fallen in love with him. For all I know, Celia may have fallen in love with me. In any case, the Reverend and I were clearly unavailable.

As only a gifted actor could, the Reverend made the Mask and Wig Club's production of *Katmandu,* and especially Celia's performance, sound as though it had enriched lives all over town. My own calculation is that people were as moved by the play as they might have been by a good game of basketball. The auditorium was a nice enough place to be that night.

• • •

Reverend Harrell said it was sad that Celia had not lived to see the completion of the Mildred Barry Memorial Center for the Arts in Sugar Creek, but that her performance in *Katmandu* was proof that the arts were important in Midland City before the center was built.

He declared that the most important arts centers a city could have were human beings, not buildings. He called attention to me again. "There in the back sits an arts center named 'Rudy Waltz,' " he said.

It was then that Felix and his friend methaqualone began wailing. Felix was as loud as a fire engine, and he could not stop.

25

THERE WAS just a prayer and some music after that, thank God, and then the recessional, with the pallbearers wheeling the casket out to the hearse. Otherwise, Felix's sobbing could have wrecked the funeral. Mother and I gave up on going to the burial. We had no thought but to get Felix out of the church and into the County Hospital. It was all we could do not to get out ahead of the casket.

We had come late, so we were parked fairly far out on the parking lot, and there were a number of neighborhood children paying their respects to the Rolls-Royce. They had never seen one before, I'm sure, but they knew what it was. They were so reverent, that they might have been attending an open-casket funeral right there in the parking lot.

Celia Hoover's casket, by the way, was closed. That must have been because of the Drāno.

We got Felix into the back seat without any trouble. He sat there with the top down, sobbing away. I think we could have sent him up a tree, and he would have been up among the branches and birds' nests, sobbing away.

But he wouldn't give us the keys. The keys were too materialistic a concern for him to consider at such a time. So I had to go through his pockets, while Mother told me to hurry up, hurry up. I happened to glance in the direction of the church, and I saw that Dwayne Hoover, maybe having told everybody to stay behind, that he had some private business with Felix to conduct, was coming in our direction.

He might have been expected to remain close to the hearse, and to duck curious and possibly accusing eyes by getting into the undertaker's Cadillac limousine behind it. But, no—he was going to trudge fifty yards out into the parking lot instead, and we were the only people out there, since we had fled the church so quickly. So it was like a scene in a cowboy movie, with the townspeople all huddled together, and with a half-broken, tragic, great big man going to meet destiny all alone.

The hearse could wait.

He had business to settle first.

. . .

If this confrontation scene were done as a playlet, the set could be very simple. A curb along the back of the stage might indicate the edge of a parking lot. A Rolls-Royce with its top down, which is the expensive part, could be parked next to that, aimed left. Flats behind the curb could be painted with trees and shrubbery. A tasteful wooden sign might make the location more specific, saying:

FIRST METHODIST CHURCH
VISITORS' PARKING
ALL PERSONS WELCOME.

Felix would be sobbing in the back seat of the Rolls-Royce. Mother, whose name was Emma, and I, whose name is Rudy, would be between the convertible and the audience. Emma would have the heebie-jeebies, wanting to get out of there, and Rudy would be frisking Felix for the keys.

FELIX: Who cares about the keys?
EMMA: Hurry up—oh, please hurry up.
RUDY: How many pockets can they put in a London suit? God damn it, Felix.
FELIX: You're making me sorry I came home.
EMMA: I could die.
FELIX: I loved her so much.
RUDY: Did you ever!

(RUDY *happens to look in the direction of the church, off right, and is appalled to see* DWAYNE *approaching.*)

RUDY: Oh, my God.
FELIX: Pray for her. That's what I'm going to do.
RUDY: Felix—get out of the car.

EMMA: Let him stay there. Get him to hunker down.

RUDY: Mother—look behind you. Here comes Dwayne.

(EMMA *looks, hates what she sees.*)

EMMA: Oh. You'd think he'd stay with the body.

RUDY: Felix—get out of the car, because I think somebody just might want to beat the shit out of you.

FELIX: I just got home.

RUDY: I'm not kidding. Here comes Dwayne. He beat the
shit out of Doctor Mitchell a week ago. This could be
your turn.

FELIX: I've got to fight him?

RUDY: Get out of the car and run!

(FELIX *gets out of the car, muttering and complaining. His tears
have abated some. The danger is so unreal to him that he doesn't
even look to see where the danger may be coming from. He is
distracted by the dent and scratch on the side of the car as*
DWAYNE *enters right and stops.*)

FELIX: Oh, look at that. What a shame.

DWAYNE: It really is—a beautiful machine like that.

(FELIX *straightens up and turns to look at him.*)

FELIX: Hello. You're the husband.

DWAYNE: Where do you fit in?

FELIX: What?

DWAYNE: I'm the husband, and I never felt worse in my
life—but I couldn't cry the way you cried. I never
heard anybody cry like you did, male or female.
Where do you fit in?

FELIX: We were sweethearts in high school.

(As DWAYNE *thinks this over,* FELIX *takes a bottle of pills from a pocket and starts to open it.)*

EMMA: No more pills!

RUDY: My brother isn't well.

EMMA: He's insane—and I used to be so proud of him.

DWAYNE: I'd be sorry to believe he was crazy. I'm hoping
    he was crying because he was sane.

EMMA: He can't fight. He never could.

RUDY: We're on our way to the hospital.

FELIX: Just a damn minute here. I was crying because I'm
    sane. I'm the sanest person in this whole shit-storm!
    What the hell's going on?

EMMA: Go ahead and get your brains beat out.

FELIX: You must be the worst mother a person ever had.

EMMA: I never disgraced myself and my family in public,
    I'll tell you that.

FELIX: You never sewed on a button, either. You never
    hugged or kissed me.

EMMA: Who could blame me?

FELIX: You never did anything a mother's supposed to do.

DWAYNE: Just tell me more about why you cried!

FELIX: We were raised by servants—do you know that?
    This lady here ought to get switches and coal every
    Mother's Day! My brother and I know so much
    about black people and so little about white people,
    we should be in a minstrel show.

DWAYNE: He really is crazy, isn't he?

FELIX: Amos 'n' Andy.

EMMA: I have never been so humiliated in my life, and as a younger woman I have traveled all over this world.

DWAYNE: At least you never had a wife commit suicide. Or a husband.

EMMA: I know you've been through so much, and then all this on top of it.

DWAYNE: I don't know what part of the world you could have visited, where having the person you were married to commit suicide wasn't the most humiliating thing that could happen.

EMMA: You go back to your friends. And again, I'm so ashamed of my son, I wish he were dead. Go back to your friends.

DWAYNE: Those people back there? You know something? I think maybe I would have come walking out here alone, even if you hadn't been out here. If you hadn't given me a logical place to stop, I might have kept walking until I was in Katmandu. I'm the only person in town who hasn't been to Katmandu. My dentist's been to Katmandu.

EMMA: You go to Herb Stacks, too?

DWAYNE: Sure. Celia, too—or used to.

EMMA: I wonder why we never met there?

FELIX: Because he uses Gleem toothpaste with Fluoristan.

EMMA: I can't be responsible for what he says. I can't imagine how he got control of an entire major television network.

DWAYNE: Celia never told me that you and she were

sweethearts. That was her big complaint right up to the end, you know—that nobody had ever loved her, so why should she even go to the dentist anymore?

EMMA: Radio, too. He was also in charge of radio.

FELIX: You're interrupting an important conversation—as usual. Mr. Hoover—yes, Celia and I were not only sweethearts in high school, but I realized there in church that she was the only woman I had ever loved, and maybe the only woman I will ever love. I hope I have not offended you.

DWAYNE: I'm glad. I may not look glad, but I am glad. They're going to honk the horn of the hearse any minute—to tell me to hurry up, that the cemetery's about to close. She was like this Rolls-Royce here, you know?

FELIX: The most beautiful woman I ever knew. No offense, no offense.

DWAYNE: No offense. Anybody who wants to can say she was the most beautiful woman he ever saw. You should have married her, not me.

FELIX: I wasn't worthy of her. Look at the dent I put in the Rolls-Royce.

DWAYNE: You scraped up against something blue.

FELIX: Listen. She lasted a lot longer with you than she would have lasted with me. I'm one of the worst husbands there ever was.

DWAYNE: Not as bad as me. I just ran away from her, she was so unhappy, and I didn't know what to do about it—and there wasn't anybody else to take her off my hands. I'm good for selling cars. I can really sell cars. I can fix cars. I can really fix cars. But I sure couldn't fix that woman. Never even knew where to get the tools. I put her up on blocks and forgot her. I only wish you'd come along in time to rescue the both of us. But you did me a big favor today. At least I don't have to think my poor wife went all the way through life without finding out what love was.

FELIX: Where am I? What have I said? What have I done?

DWAYNE: You come on along to the cemetery. I don't care if you're crazy or not. You'll make this automobile dealer feel a little bit better, if you'll just cry some more—while we put my poor wife in the ground.

(Curtain.)

26

We all see our lives as stories, it seems to me, and I am convinced that psychologists and sociologists and historians and so on would find it useful to acknowledge that. If a person survives an ordinary span of sixty years or more, there is every chance that his or her life as a shapely story has ended, and all that remains to be experienced is epilogue. Life is not over, but the story is.

Some people, of course, find inhabiting an epilogue so uncongenial that they commit suicide. Ernest Hemmingway comes to mind. Celia Hoover, née Hildreth, comes to mind.

My own father's story ended, it seems to me, and it must have seemed to him, when he took all the blame for my having shot Eloise Metzger—and then the police threw him down the iron staircase. He could not be an artist, and he could not be a soldier—but he could at least be heroically honorable and truthful, should an opportunity to be so present itself.

235

That was the story of his life which he carried in his head.

The opportunity presented itself. He was heroically honorable and truthful. He was thrown down the staircase—like so much garbage.

It was then that these words should have appeared somewhere:

THE END.

But they didn't. But his life as a story was over anyway. The remaining years were epilogue—a sort of junk shop of events which were nothing more than random curiosities, boxes and bins of whatchamacallits.

This could be true of nations, too. Nations might think of themselves as stories, and the stories end, but life goes on. Maybe my own country's life as a story ended after the Second World War, when it was the richest and most powerful nation on earth, when it was going to ensure peace and justice everywhere, since it alone had the atom bomb.

THE END.

Felix likes this theory a lot. He says that his own life as a story ended when he was made president of the National Broadcasting Company, and was celebrated as one of the ten best-dressed men in the country.

THE END.

He says, though, that his epilogue rather than his story has been the best part of his life. This must often be the case.

Bernard Ketchum told us about one of Plato's dialogues, in which an old man is asked how it felt not to be excited by sex anymore. The old man replies that it was like being allowed to dismount from a wild horse.

Felix says that that was certainly how he felt when he was canned by NBC.

• • •

It may be a bad thing that so many people try to make good stories out of their lives. A story, after all, is as artificial as a mechanical bucking bronco in a drinking establishment.

And it may be even worse for nations to try to be characters in stories.

Perhaps these words should be carved over doorways of the United Nations and all sorts of parliaments, big and small: LEAVE YOUR STORY OUTSIDE.

• • •

I got off the wild horse of my own life story at Celia Hoover's funeral, I think—when Reverend Harrell forgave me in public for having shot Eloise Metzger so long ago. If it wasn't then, it was only a couple of years after that, when Mother was finally killed by the radioactive mantelpiece.

I had paid her back as best I could for ruining her life and Father's. She was no longer in need of personal services. The case was closed.

. . .

We probably never would have found out that it was the mantelpiece that killed her, if it weren't for an art historian from Ohio University over at Athens. His name was Cliff McCarthy. He was a painter, too. And Cliff McCarthy never would have got involved in our lives, if it hadn't been for all the publicity Mother received for objecting to the kind of art Fred T. Barry was buying for the arts center. He read about her in *People* magazine. Then again, Mother almost certainly wouldn't have become so passionate about taking Fred T. Barry on in the first place, if it hadn't been for little tumors in her brain, which had been caused by the radioactive mantelpiece.

Wheels within wheels!

People magazine described Mother as the widow of an Ohio painter. Cliff McCarthy had been working for years, financed by a Cleveland philanthropist, on a book which was to include every serious Ohio painter, but he had never heard of Father. So he visited our little shitbox, and he photographed Father's unfinished painting over the fireplace. That was all there was to photograph, so he took several exposures of that with a big camera on a tripod. He was being polite, I guess.

But the camera used flat packs of four-by-five film,

and he had exposed some of it elsewhere, so he got several packs out of his camera bag.

He accidentally left one behind—on the mantelpiece. One week later he swung off the Interstate, on his way to someplace else, and he picked up the pack.

Three days after that, he called me on the telephone to say that the film in the pack had all turned black, and that a friend of his who taught physics had offered the opinion that the film had been close to something which was highly radioactive.

· · ·

He gave me another piece of news on the telephone, too. He had been looking at a diary kept by the great Ohio painter Frank Duveneck at the end of his life. He died in 1919, at the age of seventy-one. Duveneck spent his most productive years in Europe, but he returned to his native Cincinnati after his wife died in Florence, Italy.

"Your father is in the diary!" said McCarthy. "Duveneck heard about this wonderful studio a young painter was building in Midland City, and on March 16, 1915, he went and had a look at it."

"What did he say?" I asked.

"He said it was certainly a beautiful studio, such as any artist in the world would have given his eyeteeth to have."

"I mean, what did he say about Father?" I said.

"He liked him, I think," said McCarthy.

"Look," I said, "—I'm aware that my father was a fraud, and Father knew it, too. Duveneck was probably the only really important painter who ever saw Father's masquerade. No matter how cutting it is, please tell me what Duveneck said."

"Well—I'll read it to you," said McCarthy, and he did: " 'Otto Waltz should be shot. He should be shot for seeming to prove the last thing that needs to be proved in this part of the world: that an artist is a person of no consequence.' "

. . .

I asked around about who was in charge of civil defense. I hoped that whoever it was would have a Geiger counter, or some other method of measuring radioactivity. It turned out that the director of civil defense for the county was Lowell Ulm, who owned the car wash on the Shepherdstown Turnpike by the airport. He was who you were supposed to call in case of World War Three. He did have a Geiger counter.

So he came over after work. He had to go home for the Geiger counter first. That innocent-looking mantelpiece, before which Mother had spent so many hours, either gazing into the flames or up at Father's unfinished painting, was a killer. Lowell Ulm said this: "Jesus Christ! This thing is hotter than a Hiroshima baby carriage!"

. . .

Mother and I were moved into the new Holiday Inn, while workmen dressed like astronauts on the moon performed radical surgery on our little Avondale shitbox. The irony was, of course, that, if Mother had been a typical mother, out in the kitchen or down in the basement or out shopping most of the time, and if I had been a typical son, waiting to be fed, and lounging around the living room, I would have been the one to get the fatal dose of radiation.

At least Gino and Marco Maritimo were both dead by then, presumably feeling nothing. They would have been heartsick to learn that the house which they had practically given to us was so dangerous. Marco had his peephole closed by natural causes about a month before Celia Hoover's funeral, and then Gino was killed in a freak accident at the arts center a few months after that. He was trying to get the center's drawbridge to work right, with the dedication ceremonies only a week away, and he was electrocuted. Two people died during the construction of the Mildred Barry Memorial Center for the Arts.

I have no idea how many people were killed during the construction of the Taj Mahal. Hundreds upon hundreds, probably. Beauty seldom comes cheap.

· · ·

But Gino and Marco's sons certainly took the mantelpiece seriously. They were as embarrassed as their fathers would have been, and they told us a lot more than they should have, since Felix and I would eventually decide to sue their corporation and a lot of other people by and by. The mantelpiece, they told us, came from a scrap heap in weeds back of an ornamental concrete company outside of Cincinnati. Old Gino had found it there, and couldn't see anything wrong with it, and had bought it cheap for the model house, which became our house, at Avondale.

With a lot of luck, and the help of a few honest people, we were able to trace the cement that went into the mantelpiece all the way back to Oak Ridge, Tennessee, where pure uranium 235 was produced for the bomb they dropped on Hiroshima in 1945. The government somehow allowed that cement to be sold off as war surplus, even though many people had known how hot it was.

In this case, the government was about as careless as a half-wit boy up in a cupola with a loaded Springfield rifle—on Mother's Day.

• • •

When Mother and I moved back into our little shitbox, we didn't have a fireplace anymore. We had been away for only twenty-four hours, but a Sheetrock wall had replaced the fireplace, and the whole living room had been repainted. The Maritimo Brothers Construction Company had done all that at their own expense. It wasn't even possible to tell that we had once had a fireplace.

Felix wasn't around to see the transformation. He had taken a job under an assumed name, although his employers knew who he really was, or who he really had been, as an announcer on a radio station in South Bend, Indiana.

This wasn't a humiliation. It was what he wanted to do, what he said he had been born to do. He was drug free. We were so proud of him.

• • •

Mother said a significant thing when she saw we didn't have a fireplace anymore. "Oh, dear—I don't know if I want to go on living without a fireplace."

"What part of her life," you might ask, "was story, and what part was epilogue?" I think her case was similar to Father's, in that, by the time my brother and I came along, there was nothing left but epilogue. The circumstances of her early life virtually decreed that she live only a pipsqueak story, which was over only a few moments after it had begun. She had nothing to atone for, for example, since she was never tempted to do anything bad in the first place. And she wasn't going to go seeking any kind of Holy Grail, since that was clearly a man's job, and she already had a cup that overflowed and overflowed with good things to eat and drink anyway.

I suppose that's really what so many American women are complaining about these days: They find their lives short on story and overburdened with epilogue.

Mother's story ended when she married the handsomest rich man in town.

27

Mother said that thing about not knowing if she wanted to go on living, if she couldn't have a fireplace—and then the telephone rang. Mother answered. I used to be the one to answer the telephone, but now she always beat me to it. Almost every call was thrillingly for her, since she had become the local Saint Joan of Arc in a holy war against nonrepresentational art.

A year had passed since the dedication of the Mildred Barry Memorial Center for the Arts, with speeches and performances by noted creative persons from all over the country. Now it was virtually as empty and unvisited as the old Sears, Roebuck downtown, or the railroad station, where the Monon and New York Central railroads used to intersect, but which didn't even have tracks anymore.

Mother had been bounced off the board of directors of the center, for her disruptive behavior at meetings, and for her unfriendly comments on the center in the press and before church groups and garden clubs and so on. She was much in demand as a sparkling, prickly public speaker.

Fred T. Barry, for his part, had become as silent as the center itself. I saw his Lincoln limousine a couple of times, but the back windows were opaque, so I have no idea whether he was in there or not. I would see his company jet parked out at the airport sometimes, but never him. I expected to hear news of Mr. Barry from time to time, as in the past, from employees of his who happened into the drugstore. But then it became evident that Mr. Barry's employees were boycotting Schramm's Drugstore, both night and day, because my mother's younger son was an employee there.

So it was a surprise that Mother now found herself talking on the telephone to none other than Fred T. Barry. He hoped, with all possible courtliness, that Mother would be home during the next hour, and willing to receive him. He had never been in our little shitbox before. I doubt, in fact, that he had ever before been in Avondale.

Mother told him to come ahead. Those were her exact words, delivered in the flat tones of someone who had never lost a fight: "Come ahead, if you want to."

• • •

Mother and I had not yet begun to speculate seriously about what the radioactive mantelpiece might have done to our health, nor had we been encouraged to do so. Nor would we ever be encouraged to do so. Ulm, the director of civil defense and car-wash tycoon, had been getting advice on our case over the telephone from somebody at the Nuclear Regulatory Commission in Washington,

D.C., to the effect that the most important thing was that nobody panic. In order to prevent panic, the workmen who had torn out our fireplace, wearing protective clothing provided by Ulm, had been sworn to secrecy—in the name of patriotism, of national security.

The cover story, provided by Washington, D.C., and spread throughout Avondale while Mother and I were staying at the new Holiday Inn, was that our house had been riddled by termites, and that the protective clothing was necessary, since the workmen had killed the insects with cyanide.

Insects.

So we did not panic. Good citizens don't. We waited calmly for Fred T. Barry. I was at the picture window, peering out at the street between slats of the Venetian blinds. Mother was reclining in the Barcalounger my brother Felix had given her three Christmases ago. She was vibrating almost imperceptibly, and a reassuring drone came from underneath her. She had the massage motor turned on low.

Mother said that she didn't feel any different, now that she knew she had been exposed to radioactivity. "Do you feel any different?" she asked.

"No," I said. This sort of conversation is going to become increasingly common, I think, as radioactive materials get spread around the world.

"If we were in such great danger," she said, "you'd think we would have noticed something. There would have been dead bugs on the mantelpiece, don't you think—or the plants would have gotten funny spots or something?"

Meanwhile, little tumors were blooming in her head.

"I'm so sorry they told the neighbors we had termites," she said. "I wish they could have thought of something else. It's like telling everybody we had leprosy."

It turned out that she had had a traumatic experience with termites in childhood, which she had never mentioned to me. She had suppressed the memory all those years, but now she told me, full of horror, of walking into the music room of her father's mansion, which she had believed to be so indestructible when she was a little girl, and seeing what looked like foam, boiling out the floor and a baseboard near the grand piano, and out of the legs and the keyboard of the piano itself.

"There were billions and billions of bugs with shiny wings, acting for all the world like a liquid," she said. "I ran and got Father. He couldn't believe his eyes, either. Nobody had played the piano for years. If somebody had played it, maybe it would have driven the bugs out of there. Father gave a piano leg a little kick, and it crumpled like it was made out of cardboard. The piano fell down."

. . .

This was clearly one of the most memorable events of her whole life, and I had never heard of it before.

If she had died in childhood, she would have remembered life as the place you went, in case you wanted to see bugs eat a grand piano.

• • •

So Fred T. Barry arrived in his limousine. He was so old now, and Mother was so old now, and they had had this long fight about whether modern art was any good or not. I let him in, and Mother received him while lying on the Barcalounger.

"I have come to surrender, Mrs. Waltz," he said. "You should be very proud of yourself. I have lost all interest in the arts center. It can be turned into a chicken coop, for all I care. I am leaving Midland City forever."

"I am sure you had the best intentions, Mr. Barry," she said. "I never doubted that. But the next time you try to give somebody a wonderful present, make sure they want it first. Don't try to stuff it down their throats."

He sold his company to the RAMJAC Corporation for a gazoolian bucks. A firm that acquires American farmland for Arabs bought his farm. As far as I know, no Arab has ever come to take a look at it. He himself moved to Hilton Head, South Carolina, and I have heard nothing about him since. He was so bitter that he left no endowment behind to maintain the arts center, and the city was so broke that it could only let the place go to rack and ruin.

And then, one day, there was this flash.

• • •

Mother died a year after Fred T. Barry surrendered to her. When she was in the hospital for the last time, she thought she was in a spaceship. She thought I was Father, and that we were headed for Mars, where we were going to have a second honeymoon.

She was as alive as anybody, and utterly mistaken about everything. She wouldn't let go of my hand.

"That picture," she said, and she would smile and give my hand a squeeze. I was supposed to know which of all the pictures in the world she meant. I thought for a while that it was Father's unfinished masterpiece from his misspent youth in Vienna. But in a moment of clarity, she made it clear that it was a scrapbook photograph of her in a rowboat on a small river somewhere, maybe in Europe. Then again, it could have been Sugar Creek. The boat is tied to shore. There aren't any oars in place. She isn't going anywhere. She wears a summer dress and a garden hat. Somebody has persuaded her to pose in the boat, with water around her and dappled with shade. She is laughing. She has just been married, or is about to be married.

She will never be happier. She will never be more beautiful.

Who could have guessed that that young woman would take a rocket-ship trip to Mars someday?

• • •

She was seventy-seven when she died, so that all sorts of things, including plain old life, could have closed her peephole. But the autopsy revealed that she had been healthy as a young horse, except for tumors in her head. Tumors of that sort, moreover, could only have been caused by radiation, so Felix and I hired Bernard Ketchum to sue everybody who had bought or sold in any form the radioactive cement from Oak Ridge.

It took a while to win, and I meanwhile kept going to work six nights a week at Schramm's Drugstore, and keeping house in the little shitbox out in Avondale. There isn't all that much difference between keeping house for two and keeping house for one.

My Mercedes continued to give me an indecent amount of pleasure.

At one point there, through a misunderstanding, I was suspected of abducting and murdering a little girl. So the state police scientists impounded the Mercedes, and they went over it inch by inch with fingerprint powder and a vacuum cleaner and so on. When they gave it back to me, along with a clean bill of health, they said they had never seen anything like it. The car was seven years old then, and had over a hundred thousand miles on it, but every hair in it and every fingerprint on it belonged to just one person, the owner.

"You aren't what we would call real sociable," one trooper said. "How come you got a car with four doors?"

• • •

Polka-dot brownies: Melt half a cup of butter and a pound of light-brown sugar in a two-quart saucepan. Stir over a low fire until just bubbly. Cool to room temperature. Beat in two eggs and a teaspoon of vanilla. Stir in a cup of sifted flour, a half teaspoon of salt, a cup of chopped filberts, and a cup of semisweet chocolate in small chunks.

Spread into a well-greased nine-by-eleven baking pan. Bake at two hundred and thirty-five degrees for about thirty-five minutes.

Cool to room temperature, and cut into squares with a well-greased knife.

. . .

I think I was about as happy as anybody else in Midland City, and maybe in the country, as I waited for all the lawsuits to come to a head. But there you have a problem in relativity again. I continued to be comforted by music of my own making, the scat singing, the brainless inward fusillades of "skeedee wahs" and "bodey oh dohs," and so on. I had a Blaupunkt FM-AM stereophonic radio in my Mercedes, but I hardly ever turned it on.

As for scat singing: I came across what I consider a most amusing graffito, written in ball-point pen on tile in the men's room at Will Fairchild Memorial Airport one morning. It was dawn, and I was seized by an attack of diarrhea on my way home from work, just as I was passing the airport. It was caused, I'm sure, by my having eaten so many polka-dot brownies before going to work the night before.

So I swung into the airport, and jumped out of my four-door Mercedes. I didn't expect to get into the building. I just wanted to get out of sight. But there was another car in the parking lot at that unlikely hour. So I tried a side door, and it was unlocked.

In I flew, and up to the men's room, noting in flight

that somebody was running a floor-waxing machine. I relieved myself, and became as calm and respectable as any other citizen again, or even more so. For a few moments there, I was happier than happy, healthier than healthy, and I saw these words scrawled on the tiles over a wash basin:

"To be is to do"—Socrates.
"To do is to be"—Jean-Paul Sartre.
"Do be do be do"—Frank Sinatra.

EPILOGUE

I HAVE NOW SEEN with my own eyes what a neutron bomb can do to a small city. I am back at the Hotel Oloffson after three days in my old hometown. Midland City was exactly as I remembered it, except that there were no people living there. The security is excellent. The perimeter of the flash area is marked by a high fence topped with barbed wire, with a watchtower every three hundred yards or so. There is a minefield in front of that, and then a low barbed wire entanglement beyond that, which wouldn't stop a truly determined person, but which is meant as a friendly warning about the mines.

It is possible for a civilian to visit inside the fence only in daylight. After nightfall, the flash area becomes a free-fire zone. Soldiers are under orders to shoot anything that moves, and their weapons are equipped with infrared sights. They can see in the dark.

And in the daytime, the only permissible form of

transportation for a civilian inside is a bright purple school bus, driven by a soldier, and with other soldiers aboard as stern and watchful guides. Nobody gets to bring his own car inside or to walk where he likes, even if he has lost his business and all his relatives and everything. It is all government property now. It belongs to all the people, instead of just some of them.

We were a party of four—Felix and myself and Bernard Ketchum, our lawyer, and Hippolyte Paul De Mille, the headwaiter from the Oloffson. Ketchum's wife and Felix's wife had declined to come along. They were afraid of radioactivity, and Felix's wife was especially afraid of it, since she was with child. We were unable to persuade those superstitious souls that the whole beauty of a neutron bomb explosion was that there was no lingering radiation afterwards.

Felix and I had run into the same sort of ignorance when it was time to bury Mother next to Father in Calvary Cemetery. People refused to believe that she herself wasn't radioactive. They were sure that she would make all the other bodies glow in the dark, and that she would seep into the water supply and so on.

For Mother to be personally radioactive, she would have had to bite a piece out of the mantelpiece, and then fail to excrete it. If she had done that, it's true, she would have been a holy terror for twenty thousand years or more.

But she didn't.

. . .

We brought old Hippolyte Paul De Mille along, who had never been outside Haiti before, on the pretext that he was the brother of a Haitian cook for Dr. Alan Maritimo, the veterinarian, and his wife. Alan was a maverick in the Maritimo family, who had declined to go into the building business. His entire household was killed by the flash. Ketchum had put together fake affidavits which entitled Hippolyte Paul to pass through the gate in a purple school bus with the rest of us.

We went to this trouble for Hippolyte Paul because he was our most valuable employee. Without him and his goodwill, the Grand Hotel Oloffson would have been a worthless husk. It was worth our while to keep him happy.

But Hippolyte Paul, in his excitement about the trip, had volunteered to make us a highly specific gift, which we intended to refuse politely at the proper time. He said that if there was any ghost we thought should haunt Midland City for the next few hundred years, he would raise it from its grave and turn it loose, to wander where it would.

We tried very hard not to believe that he could do that.

But he could, he could.

Amazing.

• • •

There was no odor. We expected a lot of odor, but there was none. Army engineers had buried all the dead under the block-square municipal parking lot across the street from police headquarters, where the old courthouse

257

had stood. They had then repaved the lot, and put the dwarf arboretum of parking meters back in place. The whole process had been filmed, we were told—from parking lot to mass grave, and then back to parking lot again.

My brother Felix, in that rumbling voice of his, speculated that a flying saucer might someday land on the mass grave, and conclude that the whole planet was asphalt, and that parking meters were the only living things. We were sitting in a school bus. We weren't allowed to get out at that point.

"Maybe it will look like the Garden of Eden to some bug-eyed monsters," Felix went on. "They will love it. They will crack open the parking meters with the butts of their zap-pistols, and they will feast on all the slugs and beer-can tops and coins."

• • •

We caught sight of several movie crews, and they were given as the reason we weren't to touch anything, even though it might unquestionably have been our own property. It was as though we were in a national park, full of endangered species. We weren't even to pick a little flower to sniff. It might be the very last such flower anywhere.

When our school bus took us to Mother's and my little shitbox out in Avondale, for example, I wandered to the Meekers' house next door. Young Jimmy Meeker's tricycle, with white sidewall tires, was sitting in the driveway, waiting patiently for its master. I put my hand on the seat, meaning to roll it back and forth just a few inches, and to wonder what life in Midland City had been all about.

And such a yell I heard!

Captain Julian Pefko, who was in charge of our party, yelled at me, "Hands in your pockets!" That was one of the rules: Whenever men were outside the school bus, they were to keep their hands in their pockets. Women, if they had pockets, were to do the same. If they didn't have pockets, they were to keep their arms folded across their bosoms. Pefko reminded me that we were under martial law as long as we were inside the fence. "One more dumb trick like that, mister," he told me, "and you're on your way to the stockade. How would you like twenty years on the rockpile?" he said.

"I wouldn't, sir," I said. "I wouldn't like that at all."

And there wasn't any more trouble after that. We certainly all behaved ourselves. You can learn all kinds of habits quickly under martial law.

The reason everything had to be left exactly where it was, of course, was so that camera crews could document, without the least bit of fakery, the fundamental harmlessness of a neutron bomb.

Skeptics would be put to flight, once and for all.

• • •

The empty city did not give me the creeps, and Hippolyte Paul actually enjoyed it. He didn't miss the people, since he had no people to miss. Limited to the present tense, he kept exclaiming in Creole, "How rich they are! How rich they are!"

But Felix finally found my serenity something to complain about. "Jesus Christ!" he exploded as our second afternoon in the flash area was ending. "Would you show just a trace of emotion, please?"

So I told him, "This isn't anything I haven't seen on practically every day of my adult life. The sun is setting instead of rising—but otherwise this is what Midland City always looked like and felt like to me when I locked up Schramm's Drugstore at dawn:

"Everybody has left town but me."

. . .

We were allowed into Midland City in order to photograph and make lists of all the items of personal property which were certainly ours, or which might be ours, or which we thought we might inherit, once all the legal technicalities were unscrambled. As I say, we weren't allowed to actually touch anything. The penalty for trying to smuggle anything out of the flash area, no matter how worthless, was twenty years in prison for civilians. For soldiers, the penalty was death.

As I say, the security was quite wonderful, and we heard many visitors who had certainly been more horribly bereaved than we were praise the military for its smart appearance and efficiency. It was almost as though Midland

City were at last being run the way it should have been run all along.

But, as we were to discover on the morning of our third and final day, where the minefield outside the fence ended, highly treasonous opinion of the Federal Government began. The farmers on the fringe of the flash area, in the past as politically inert as mastodons, had been turned into bughouse social commentators by the flash.

They had lost their shopping centers, of course.

So Felix and I and Ketchum and Hippolyte Paul were having breakfast at the Quality Motor Court out by Sacred Miracle Cave, where we were staying, and where our purple school bus would pick us up, and two farmers in bib overalls, just like old John Fortune in Katmandu, were passing out leaflets in the coffee shop. The Quality Motor Court was not then under martial law. I understand that all motels within fifty miles of Midland City have now been placed under martial law.

These two said the same thing over and over again as they offered their leaflets: "Read the truth and then write your congressman." About half the customers refused to even look at the leaflets, but we each took one.

The organization which wanted us to write our congressmen, it turned out, was "Farmers of Southwestern Ohio for Nuclear Sanity." They said that it was all well and good that the Federal Government should be making idealistic plans for Midland City, as a haven for refugees from less fortunate countries or whatever. But they also felt that there should be some public discussion, that "the veil of silence should be lifted" from the mystery of how all the previous inhabitants had wound up under the municipal parking lot.

They confessed that they were fighting a losing battle in trying to make anybody outside of southwestern Ohio care what had happened to someplace called "Midland City." As far as the farmers knew, Midland City had never even been mentioned on a major network television show until after the flash. They were wrong about that, incidentally. It was certainly network news during the Blizzard of 1960, but I can't remember any other time. Power went off during the blizzard, so the farmers had no way of knowing that Midland City had finally made the TV.

They missed it!

But that didn't weaken the argument of their leaflet, to wit: that the United States of America was now ruled, evidently, by a small clique of power brokers who believed that most Americans were so boring and ungifted and small time that they could be slain by the tens of thousands without inspiring any long-term regrets on the part of anyone. "They have now proved this with Midland City," said the leaflet, "and who is to say that Terre Haute or Schenectady will not be next?"

That was certainly the most inflammatory of their beliefs—that Midland City had been neutron-bombed on purpose, and not from a truck, but from a missile site or a high-flying airplane. They had hired a mathematician from, they said, "a great university," to make calculations independent of the Government's, as to where the flash had originated. The mathematician could not be named, they said, for fear that retaliatory action would be taken against him, but it was his opinion, based largely on the pattern of livestock deaths on the outer perimeter of the flash, that the center of the flash was near Exit 11 on the Interstate, all right, but at least sixty feet above the pavement. That certainly suggested a package which had arrived by air.

Either that, or a truck had been hauling a neutron bomb in an enormous pop-up toaster.

. . .

Bernard Ketchum asked the farmer who had given us our leaflets to name the clique which had supposedly neutron-bombed Midland City. This was the answer he got: "They don't want us to know their name, so they don't have a name. You can't fight back against something that don't have a name."

"The military-industrial complex?" said Ketchum archly. "The Rockefellers? The international conglomerates? The CIA? The Mafia?"

And the farmer said to him, "You like any of them names? Just help yourself. Maybe that's who it is, maybe it ain't. How's a farmer supposed to find out? It's whoever it was shot President Kennedy and his brother—and Martin Luther King."

So there we had it—the ever-growing ball of American paranoia, the ball of string a hundred miles in diameter, with the unsolved assassination of John F. Kennedy at its core.

"You mention the Rockefellers," said the farmer. "If you ask me, they don't know any more'n I do about who's really running things, what's really going on."

• • •

Ketchum asked him why these nameless, invisible forces would want to depopulate Midland City—and then maybe Terre Haute and Schenectady after that.

"Slavery!" was the farmer's prompt reply.

"I beg your pardon?" said Ketchum.

"They aim to bring slavery back," said the farmer. He wouldn't tell us his name, for fear of reprisals, but I had a hunch he was an Osterman. There were several Ostermans with farms out around Sacred Miracle Cave.

"They never gave up on it," he said. "The Civil War wasn't going to make any difference in the long run, as far as they were concerned. Sooner or later, they knew in their hearts, we'd get back to owning slaves."

Ketchum said jocularly that he could understand the desirability of a slave economy, especially in view of all the trouble so many American industries were having with foreign competition. "But I fail to see the connection between slaves and empty cities," he said.

"What we figure," said the farmer: "These slaves aren't going to be Americans. They're going to come by the boatload from Haiti and Jamaica and places like that, where there's such terrible poverty and overpopulation. They're going to need housing. What's cheaper—to use what we've already got, or to build new?"

He let us think that over for a moment, and then he added, "And guess what? You've seen that fence with the watchtowers. Do you honestly believe that fence is ever coming down?"

• • •

Ketchum said he certain wished he knew who these sinister forces were.

"I'll make a wild guess," said the farmer, "and you're going to laugh at it, because the people I'll name want to be laughed at until it's too late. They don't want anybody worrying about whether they're taking over the country from top to bottom—until it's too late."

This was his wild guess: "The Ku Klux Klan."

• • •

My own guess is that the American Government had to find out for certain whether the neutron bomb was as harmless as it was supposed to be. So it set one off in a small city which nobody cared about, where people weren't doing all that much with their lives anyhow, where businesses were going under or moving away. The Government couldn't test a bomb on a foreign city, after all, without running the risk of starting World War Three.

There is even a chance that Fred T. Barry, with all his

contacts high in the military, could have named Midland City as the ideal place to test a neutron bomb.

• • •

At the end of our third day in Midland City, Felix became tearful and risked the displeasure of Captain Julian Pefko by asking him if we could please, on the way to the main gate, have our purple school bus make a slight detour past Calvary Cemetery, so we could visit our parents' grave.

For all his rough and ready manners, Pefko, like so many professional soldiers, turned out to have an almond macaroon for a heart. He agreed.

• • •

Almond macaroons: Preheat an oven to three hundred degrees, and work one cup of confectioners' sugar into a cup of almond paste with your fingertips. Add three egg whites, a dash of salt, and a half teaspoon of vanilla.

Fit unglazed paper onto a cookie sheet. Sprinkle with granulated sugar. Force the almond paste mixture through a round pastry tube, so that uniform gobs, nicely spaced, drop onto the glazed paper. Sprinkle with granulated sugar.

Bake about twenty minutes. Tip: Put the sheet of macaroons on a damp cloth, paper side down. This will make it easier to loosen the cookies from the paper.

Cool.

• • •

Calvary Cemetery has never been any comfort to me, so I almost stayed in the purple school bus. But then, after all the others had got out, I got out, too—to stretch my legs. I strolled into the old part of the cemetery, which had been all filled up, by and large, before I was born. I stationed myself at the foot of the most imposing monument in the bone orchard, a sixty-two-foot gray marble obelisk with a stone football on top. It celebrated George Hickman Bannister, a seventeen-year-old whose peephole was closed while he was playing high school football on the morning of Thanksgiving in 1924. He was from a poor family, but thousands of people had seen him die, our parents not among them—and many of them had chipped in to buy him the obelisk.

Our parents had no interest in sports.

Maybe twenty feet away from the obelisk was the most fanciful marker in the cemetery, a radial, air-cooled airplane engine reproduced in pink marble, and fitted with a bronze propeller. This was the headstone of Will Fairchild, the World War One ace in the Lafayette Escadrille, after whom the airport was named. He hadn't died in the war. He had crashed and burned, again with thousands watching, in 1922, while stunt flying at the Midland County Fair.

He was the last of the Fairchilds, a pioneering family after which so much in the city was named. He had failed to reproduce before his peephole closed.

Inscribed in the bronze propeller were his name and dates, and the euphemism fliers in the Lafayette Escadrille used for death in an airplane in wartime: "Gone West."

"West," to an American in Europe, of course, meant "home."

Here he was home.

Somewhere near me, I knew, was the headless body of old August Gunther, who had taken Father when a youth to the fanciest whorehouses in the Corn Belt. Shame on him.

I raised my eyes to the horizon, and there, on the other side of shining Sugar Creek, was the white-capped slate roof of my childhood home. In the level rays of the setting sun, it did indeed resemble a postcard picture of Fujiyama, the sacred volcano of Japan.

Felix and Ketchum were at a distance, visiting more contemporary graves. Felix would tell me later that he had managed to maintain his aplomb while visiting Mother and Father, but that he had gone all to pieces when, turning away from their markers, he discovered that he had been standing on Celia Hoover's grave.

Eloise Metzger, the woman I had shot, was also over there somewhere. I had never paid her a call.

I heard my brother go to pieces over Celia Hoover's grave, and I looked in his direction. I saw that Hippolyte Paul De Mille was attempting to cheer him up.

I was not alone, by the way. A soldier with a loaded M-16 was with me, making certain that I kept my hands in my pockets. We weren't even to touch tombstones. And

Felix and Hippolyte Paul and Bernard Ketchum also kept their hands in their pockets, no matter how much they might have wanted to gesticulate among the tombstones.

And then Hippolyte Paul De Mille said something to Felix in Creole which was so astonishing, so offensive, that Felix's grief dropped away like an iron mask. Hippolyte Paul had offered to raise the ghost of Celia Hoover from the grave, if Felix would really like to see her again.

There was a clash between two cultures, or I have never seen one.

To Hippolyte Paul, raising a spirit from a grave was the most ordinary sort of favor for a gifted metaphysician to offer a friend. He wasn't proposing to exhume a zombie, a walking corpse with dirt and rags clinging to it, and so on, a clearly malicious thing to do. He simply wanted to give Felix a misty but recognizable ghost to look at, and to talk to, although the ghost would not be able to reply to him, if that might somehow comfort him.

To Felix, it seemed that our Haitian headwaiter was offering to make him insane, for only a lunatic would gladly meet a ghost.

So these two very different sorts of human beings, their hands thrust deep into their pockets, talked past each other in a mixture of English and Creole, while Ketchum and Captain Pefko and a couple of other soldiers looked on.

Hippolyte Paul was at last so deeply hurt that he turned his back on Felix and walked away. He was coming in my direction, and I signaled with my head that he should keep coming, that I would explain the misunderstanding, that I understood his point of view as well as my brother's, and so on.

If he stayed mad at Felix, there went the Grand Hotel Oloffson.

"She doesn't feel anything. She doesn't know anything," he said to me in Creole. He meant that Celia's ghost wouldn't have caused any embarrassment or inconvenience or discomfort of any sort to Celia herself, who could feel nothing. The ghost would be nothing more than an illusion, based harmlessly on whatever Celia used to be.

"I know. I understand," I said. I explained that Felix had been upset about a lot of things lately, and that Hippolyte Paul would be mistaken to take anything Felix said too much to heart.

Hippolyte Paul nodded uncertainly, but then he brightened. He said that there was surely somebody in the cemetery that I would like to see again.

The soldier guarding us understood none of this, of course.

"You are nice," I said in Creole. "You are too generous, but I am happy as I am."

The old headwaiter was determined to work his miracle, whether we wanted it or not. He argued that we owed it both to the past and to the future to raise some sort of representative ghost which would haunt the city, no matter who lived there, for generations to come.

So, for the sake of the hotel, I told him to go ahead

and raise one, but from the part of the cemetery where we stood, where I didn't know anyone.

So he raised the ghost of Will Fairchild. The old barnstormer was wearing goggles and a white silk scarf and a black leather helmet and all, but no parachute.

I remembered what Father had told me about him one time: "Will Fairchild would be alive today, if only he had worn a parachute."

So there was Hippolyte Paul De Mille's gift to whoever was going to inhabit Midland City next: the restless ghost of Will Fairchild.

And I, Rudy Waltz, the William Shakespeare of Midland City, the only serious dramatist ever to live and work there, will now make my own gift to the future, which is a legend. I have invented an explanation of why Will Fairchild's ghost is likely to be seen roaming almost anywhere in town—in the empty arts center, in the lobby of the bank, out among the little shitboxes of Avondale, out among the luxurious homes of Fairchild Heights, in the vacant lot where the public library stood for so many years. . . .

Will Fairchild is looking for his parachute.

• • •

You want to know something? We are still in the Dark Ages. The Dark Ages—they haven't ended yet.

271